EMPTY COCOON

VIPIN BEHARI GOYAL

Made with ♥ on the Notion Press Platform
www.notionpress.com

To,

My Village Life

The Empty Cocoon

We of all people should recognize our provisional "cocoonish" condition; and yet the more we talk about redeeming culture and reclaiming America for Christ, the more one gets the impression that if we were actually given wings and bidden to fly, we would be disappointed to leave our cocoon behinduntransformed. What does that say about where our true devotion lies?

Modern Reformation
Jason Stellman's

It is better to be empty than filled. Every attempt to fill emptiness made me more hollow.The one for whom I wove this shell had walked out. I could not stop it from going. Once it was the sole purpose of my existence. Now when I am left alone I enjoy a type of freedom I never thought existed. ~Author

He had spent his whole day counting currency notes at the cash counter of a mall. After finishing his job as a cashier in the Mall when he reached his one room apartment, he was out of stamina to cook meals. When tired he boiled rice with vegetables, but today he could not muster the strength for even that. The town was in the grip of festivity and the Mall was worst affected by it. He could never understand why people spend money to buy useless things to celebrate a festival. A gift for beloved or a better domestic gadget does not improve life. He had only one hundred rupees in his pocket and he could not buy a meal in a decent restaurant with it. He would eat junk food from roadside stalls. That type of food goes well with the whisky. So first he would buy a quarter bottle of whisky. With the rest of the money he would devour street food and sleep in the pigeon hole in the name of the room.

The mall opens at nine am in the morning for the public. He would have to reach half an hour early to set the machines in order. His floor manager was very strict about it. He does not want an early bird customer to wait for the cash counter to open. After one delay he would give warning, if it is repeated he would terminate without any hesitation. No appeals. He had a waiting list of employment seekers. He would replace him by a better qualified person. So the best thing for survival was to reach in time. He had already been served with first notice.

His friend Bhola Ram from his native town, who got him this job, had already told him to maintain honesty and discipline. The cashier had to report excess and shortage of cash if any, to floor manager as soon as detected. A close watch was kept on each cash counter through cameras. He could never touch any money that was not his by right. All other money has been just metal or printed paper for him.

To spend thirteen hours in a day on cash counter, counting money and sorting mutilated or fake currency notes unnerved him. To do something that mind resists caused fatigue, and he was worn out by the end of the day. He would walk like a robot from Mall to his room. Most of the time he would sleep hungry and sometimes he would wake up at midnight due to cramps in his stomach caused by hunger. He would even chew dried pieces of old bread and swallow it with a gulp of water. He missed the meals cooked by his mother back in the town.

The first day when he reached city to join the new job, he thought he would stay with Bhola Ram. He reached at the Mall in the afternoon and Bhola introduced him to the floor manager. He was asked to join the next day. He spent his time watching how Bhola works. Bhola controlled supply on all the counters. He worked with speed and efficiency. He knew Bhola since his childhood. He played with him in the streets of their town together. At that time the grocery store of his father was doing good business. He dominated the group of his friends. Bhola was at his mercy for participating in games. He was of a lower caste.

Now he was at his mercy. Bhola brought him home in the evening and they ate meals. Bhola lived with his wife and two children in a one room apartment. After the meal, he overheard arguments between Bhola and his wife. They had no space for him to spend the night. Bhola argued that he can sleep in the open outside the house. When we went for a walk after food, he begged an excuse to spend night with some other friend. Bhola did not resist, but reminded him to reach the mall in time.

He had nowhere to go. He did not have enough money to stay even in the cheap hotel. He considered a hostel but it was too far and he did not want to get late on the first day of his job. His throat choked by thirst and he used a public tap for water. Behind the public stand post was a forlorn garden. The Mall was not far from there. He decided to spend his night on a bench in the garden. He could not sleep due to mosquitoes. He got up when it was still dark. He puts off all his clothes and took a bath under the tap of the public stand post. When his body went dry he wore the same clothes again. He combed hair with his pocket comb. The tea vendor was the first to open his kiosk. He took his morning cup of tea. The tea vendor was a friendly guy. He had seen many young men from town seeking a job in the city. He asked the vendor for a rented room. The vendor suggested a newly constructed building in the locality. He went to that building. It was close to the Mall and the rooms were very small and had a small balcony. The caretaker said the rooms are available. The rent was also nominal, but he had no money to pay an advance. He thought to take an advance from a manager or borrow from his friend, Bhola.

The first day he was asked to assist a salesman. The salesman would show the clothes made for children to the customer and he would fold back rejected piece back into boxes. Every piece had a price tag, and the prices were fixed. The customer had a price range he could afford and a budget. The salesman would convince him to exceed both. Usually he was successful. He had many arguments to convince the client and all of them were not correct, as he learned later.

After a few pegs of whisky and bellyful junk food, he was contended to have killed one more day successfully. The few coins that were left in his pocket, he donated to a beggar. The next day he would get his salary and a lease of one month to survive. Once he has paid rent and sent money to his parents, he would rest assured that his pocket is not empty by the end of the month.

Next day he could not get his salary. The boss was out and could not sign the cheque. He would come back only after three days. The landlord would not understand hie problem, he would put his bag and baggage on the road. He was a professional rent collector devoid of any emotions. His parents would be panicky, and his father might come to inquire what was wrong. So he needed five hundred rupees anyhow. He would pay two hundred rupees to landlord and send three hundred rupees through a bus conductor to his parents.

On his first day when he asked for an advance from manager he refused. They never pay an advance as a policy matter. He asked Bhola, who also made some excuse. He had to spend a complete month before he gets his salary. He can't live on water and air alone. He can sleep in the garden; thirty more nights in the garden would not kill him. He would burn some Neem leaves near his bench to scare mosquitoes. He probed possibilities. Begging was out of the question. He had nothing for sale. His digital wrist watch was not worth even a cup of tea. Working lunch was given on the Mall in packets. Can he ask for two? Can he hide one for the evening? He shivered with the thought of being caught. Everybody would know that new boy appointed was a bread thief, and he would die of shame. It is better to die of hunger than die of shame.

The wife of Bhola was also from the same town. Her name was Usha. She was a girl of lower caste like Bhola. She could hardly complete her primary education. She was married to Bhola in childhood. She was ten years old when she was withdrawn from school and sent to cater herd of She-goats. At that time he was in the final year of school with Bhola. Bhola joined job in this Mall and he went to the city to study further. He fell in company of bad boys. He learned all bad habits very quickly. His father was old and could not manage grocery shop well. Many modern departmental stores had opened in town and his father was lagging behind. Traditional grocery stores had become obsolete in town and either they were modernized or closed.

He was sacked from university for consuming alcohol and drugs in the hostel. He had already misbehaved with warden so he saw to it that he was expelled from college. He came back to town. His father asked him to get married and do some job. No good proposals were coming for him. The girl he was betrothed to in childhood was now a student of an Engineering College and had refused to marry him. Being non graduate and rusticated from college he had no job opportunity. He disliked his father's shop. His mother had sold her jewelry to sustain their life. She motivated him to do any job and live a regular life like everybody else does. Just to please her he left town and joined the job at the Mall.

To combat hunger is different than combat need of money. He was in need of temporary loans, but who could he ask. Usha came to the Mall in the afternoon with a bag. She went to the counter of fancy goods and handed her bag. The counter salesman emptied the bag on the flat glasstop of his counter. Balls of crochet laces made a heap on the counter. She collected payment from the floor manager for the goods she had supplied. When she took a turn to leave she found him before her. She was surprised and feigned annoyance. He said he needed five hundred rupees for a few days. Before she could say no, he took out a five hundred rupee note from the currency notes she was holding in her hand. She was left with a few loose currency notes in her hand. She wanted to shout, cry or snatch her money back but she could not decide. She looked at him contemptously and gave him three days time to return the money and left.

It was shameful. He had snatched money from the wife of his friend who is a lower caste woman. The relief was greater than the shame. He would return when he gets his salary. But he could not. His father was sick and was brought to the city. He had to be admitted in hospital. His mother attended him during the day, and he stayed in the hospital at night. All his money was spent on fee, tests and medicines. Bhola and his wife also came to the hospital. Usha could read his face, he had no money.

Next time when Usha came to deposit crochet laces, he looked in another direction to avoid meeting with her. She came to his counter and said she needs her money. She had to buy thread for laces and pay labor charges to women who work for her. He promised to ireturn it next month.

Next month when he received his salary he had decided to return the money even if he had to sleep hungry for the rest of the month. He had to attend the marriage of his cousin sister. As per custom he had to gift clothes and money to his sister. He bought a new dress for himself. He could hardly make his both ends meet.

Usha came to the Mall every fortnight to supply laces. Now she was direct in approach and almost rebuked him for not returning the money. She knew he was not making an excuse, but she too needed her money badly. He looked hurt when she rebuked, so he pleaded and almost begged to compensate.

He did not like money to rule his life. He had never given it so much importance. What could be more despicable? This thing was between him and Usha. They had not taken Bhola into confidence. To involve him at this stage would raise suspicion. He had tried to borrow money but Bhola was always curt so far as money was concerned.

Next time when Usha came she asked him to follow her outside. He told his peer to take care and followed her. She went to a tea stall outside Mall at a short distance. He did not join her till they were part of a small crowd at the tea stall. He offered her tea and she did not say no. She talked in slow whispering tone as if conspiring. She told him that one woman who worked for her had made a complaint to her husband that she was not paid for work done by her. Her husband had assured her that he would look into the matter. If any day he decides to check the accounts he would know that some money was missing.

Now he had started enjoying the situation. Had he returned the money, she would not have been taking tea with him without knowledge of her husband. There was a bond between them, as if they were partners in some crime. Her eyes were moist when she pleaded and he consoled her by tapping on her shoulder. While departing she held her hand and took a promise that he would return her money.

He had pretended grief but in his heart he was happy to see her in a fix. This woman who had refused to host him for a night had groveled before him.

The message reached the ears of Bhola that his wife was talking to his friend. He took it very lightly; it was not strange for people from the same town to exchange information about mutual acquaintances.

He had no idea to what extent he could exploit the situation. Usha was cunning; she had changed many colors to get her money back.

This woman was dangerous.
There was no thrill in his life; she filled an empty space.

One day before his payday, he was cooking food on the stove, when Usha dropped in unannounced on his doorsteps. He was wearing only shorts and was not in a position to get up to receive her. She hesitated a moment on the threshold, then entered. There was no chair, she remained standing. He got up, pulled trousers and a shirt on. She turned the pages of a magazine and did not look at him. Both of them sat down on the mattress. She said she had just come to remind him that tomorrow he must return her money. He said he would return it with interest. She sat awkwardly on the floor with a bent in her knees accentuating shape of her thighs. She could sense it by his stair and changed her posture. She had to readjust her long skirt when she changed her posture. A view of her white hairless calf was exposed for a few seconds.

He got up and offered her some biscuits on a plate. She picked up one and nibbled. She said her husband had stayed for overtime in Mall to arrange goods on shelves. Once in every week he does overtime and she brings his food. He works past midnight. While returning she had come to remind him. It meant she had a lot of time.

A bachelor's room is always a thing of curiosity for women. She checked his shelves. He had about a dozen books in English. He bought only those books which he could reread many times. She looked in the small mirror hung on the wall. He had a brief eye contact with her. She winked, or he thought that she winked, he was not sure.

Her presence had made the room lively. It was the first time any woman had come into his room. The room was small even for one person. In an iron trunk in the corner he kept his spare clothes.

Thankfully she did not check his trunk.
He liked people to respect his privacy.

From the beginning he had been a coward with women. In the town his friends of dominating community were fond of hunting. But he never went for hunting with his friends. They would kill a deer, cook his meat and drink wine. He liked to party with them but not the hunting. Sometimes they would pick up a shepherd girl from forest for entertainment. He never ventured into that also. He heard once they had picked up Usha, but since he was not with them he was not sure. His friends told that Usha came by her own sweet will, as she enjoyed their company.

Usha was sitting before him, totally at his mercy. He could have asked, but there was no use. Though it would be a pleasure to humiliate her further but he had no clue how to start that topic. She searched the pile of magazines and took out Vogue. Rest all were literary magazines. He was doing his under graduation in the stream of English literature, when bottles of whisky and drugs were recovered from his hostel room. If anything he missed, it was his English classes. The professor was learned and he inculcated taste for English literature in him. He did not buy Vogue; it came free with a second hand book. Usha turned each page with curiosity, she expected something more exciting.

He restarted cooking food on the stove. He ate simple vegetarian food in his daily routine. He felt difficulty in sitting squat in trousers, he had only one pair of clothes and if it is spoiled while cooking, he will feel embarrassed in the Mall. So he took off his trousers again. She had a sarcastic smile on her face. She mocked at his poverty, but he was not ashamed. To be poor is different from being ashamed of poverty.

When he finished cooking he was too hungry to wait. He invited her to eat, and she agreed. There were no spare plates so she ate with him from the same plate. She ate slowly with a delicacy, chewed without any sound or opening her mouth. It was unlike town girl who would not even drink tea without slurp. She complimented that lintel soup and vegetables were delicious. He didn't know what to say. She was frugal; when he finished eating she picked up plate and washed it with water from a bucket in the balcony. He had silver foil coated cardamom and sugar coated fennel seeds as a mouth freshener. She said she was very fond of it since childhood. She had stolen fennel seeds from her mother's small tin several times as a child.

Now when she reminisced about her childhood he asked if she had any bad experience when she took a herd of goats for grazing. She pretended to contemplate his question then affirmed that she had one terrible experience. His heart was in his throat. Now she would confess what his friends did with her. And whether she was forced or she went out of her own sweet will?

She narrated that once she went into the deep forest since all grass in open fields had been grazed. She was alone and there were none to listen even if she shouted. Her goats were thirsty. She took them to a grove where the grass was green and water was plenty. Her parents had always warned her never to go into the grove. She found that the place was enchanting. The goats were busy in grazing; she bent down near the pond to wash her face with clean water. At that time she heard rustling and hissing sounds. Before she could acknowledge the danger, a giant cobra attacked on her. She tried to shout but the sound did not come from her throat. Cobra encircled her leg with his tail and in one movement would have devoured her, had there not been a gunshot. The forest ranger was incidentally on his routine supervision and saved her life. The cobra dropped me and rushed into the forest. The ranger was annoyed with her and instructed never to come near the grove.

Was it more dangerous than attack of his friends? Could be, his friends never killed anyone. They were always searching for a fun loving girl. They would like to entice her and give her costly gifts. In rare cases if girl was beautiful, haughty and was of lower caste they would lift her from the jungle when she went to attend morning call or to graze the cattle. The parents of girl were too scared to file a complaint in the Police. It caused defamation and animosity.

Usha pushed her red bangles up in the arm to look at her wrist watch. She got up with mock concern and exclaimed that she lost sense of time. While departing she reminded him to return the money the next day.

He replied "First thing, tomorrow".

Alas! Tomorrow never comes. Despite his best intentions this time, Vicky could not return her money. After paying rent and sending money to his parents, he cleared the credit account of grocer, tea stall, phone kiosk and paid electricity bill as usual. Whisky, milk and vegetables were sold for cash only so he kept remaining five hundred rupees for that. He would give this amount to her and would survive without whisky, milk and vegetables. In the evening when he reached at his home, his gang of friends from town had come. They had come for the first time after his joining the job. They expected him to throw a party. He bought whisky and meat from the market and they cooked at home. His friends had a good capacity to consume liquor so he made it sure that there was enough for everyone. More than half of his money was spent in a single night.

When they had had few strong pegs they started boasting about their adventures with girls. The girls in town had become bolder and vagabond due to the effect of soap operas shown on television. Most of the serials on television justified extramarital relationship and free sex. The girls had started thinking that it was the culture of cities and if they would not copy, they would lag behind. On the contrary, they wanted to be bolder than their city counterparts. The boys had to encash this new wave of advancement. He casually asked about Usha, the wife of Bhola. They had to strain the memory than the chief of gang Mohan Singh spoke. She was not a joint venture of the gang. Only Mohan Singh had fancied her and she was also besotted by him, so they had few trysts before she got married.

Bhola ram and Mohan Singh were just opposite poles. If she had liked Mohan Singh before marriage, she could never like Bhola ram. Mohan Singh was the chief of our gang. He was more daring than anyone else in the group. He had a revolver and a gun. His relatives were on high posts in government and military. He was fair, tall and handsome with pointed mustache. He wore golden earrings and a black thread in neck with golden taweez. Every girl in town had a secret desire to be his beloved. The upper caste girls had lots of restrictions, even an attendant was sent with them to school. The girls of their own community were taboo; there could be big trouble. So he was left with limited choice. That is why he did not disappoint Usha when she made certain inviting gestures to him.

Bhola ram was meek and submissive. He spoke softly and apologized for minor mistakes. He was favorites of the boss. Boss gave me an appointment on his recommendation. He was first to reach and last to go from Mall. He had behaved like a wet cat before his wife. That is why he was not afraid of him. His single threat would calm him down. Even he would ask his wife to forget about money. His wife knew the weaknesses of her husband. He would never pick up a fight with his friend for five hundred rupees.

Later she came to know about visit of Mohan Singh and his friends. They had spent the money on liquor and food. She knew their priorities. Friends are more important than a promise to a woman. Mohan Singh was her first paramour. She could never forget him. He was an ideal man with whom any woman could be happy. She did not mind if he was entertained. Only if she didn't need the money to settle labor charges, she would not have insisted for payment.

After the party he was likely to get up late in the morning, he mustered all his will power to get up early and reach in time. When he left all his friends were still asleep. Two in room and two in balcony, without any space in between. He had a severe hangover. He ordered two coffees when Bhola came to his counter. He told him about the visit of Mohan Singh and other friends. Bhola's father had worked on the farm of Mohan Singh's father as labor. Bhola respected Mohan Singh.

He felt better after coffee. He wanted to go to Bhola's house and apologize to his wife for being unable to keep his promise. He asked his floor manager that he was not feeling well and wanted to take half day leave. Floor Manager looked at him. His swollen eyes, dried lips and unshaved face convinced the manager and he permitted him half day leave. He took a city bus to reach up to Bhola's house. Usha was surprised to see him. She presumed he had managed the money from his friends and had come to return. She offered him a chair to sit and brought a glass of water.

She expected him to take out money and hand it over when he said Mohan Singh came yesterday with other friends. He had to give them a party. She asked why he had taken leave just to convey a refusal. He said he was sick. In the towns people like to take care of sick people. She immediately checked his wrist and forehead for fever. He had no fever. She said it may be a cold fever, he never knew what that was. She went into the kitchen to prepare tea with clove and pepper. His hangover diminished. She asked him to lie down in bed. He protested that he would be fine. She almost dragged him to bed by holding his hand. He rested in bed. She sat down on a stool near him. She started pressing his forehead with her palm. It was considered as best service to a sick man. Her palms were fleshy and fingers were delicate. He dozed off to sleep.

The aroma of delicious food hit his nostrils. He woke up with a long yawn. Usha was in the kitchen. He said he wants to go. Usha said Bhola had come from the mall and had gone to buy sweets. He asked her what he should say about coming here. She said tell him that you were not well. He was amazed by her simplicity in cunnings.

Bhola came back with sweets. He had inquired about the absence of his friend and was told about his sickness. Bhola had visited his house and found it locked. When Bhola reached home his wife told him about his friend who was sick and how she took care of him. He was happy that his friend was well taken care of when sick.

Usha had already cooked food for him also. She served them fresh cooked chapatti swollen like a disc with lots of butter which her mother had sent from town. He had not eaten such a nice food since long time. Bhola had brought Gulab Jamun in sweets. He was surprised that Bhola remembered what he liked.

After dinner he came back to his room.

He contemplated about his relationship with Usha. He had told her that Mohan Singh had come but she did not react. May be he was not correct about Usha. Mohan Singh had a character, he would never tell a lie about his conquest on girls just to impress somebody. Has she forgotten her first paramour? No girl ever forgets. He would provoke her to come out with everything. She was vulnerable. Before he went to sleep the last thought in his mind was delicious food.

He was promoted from assistant sales man to salesman to cashier very quickly. Boss had asked for suggestions in the monthly meeting. He suggested a book counter in the mall for all age groups. Boss gave him entire responsibility to establish and manage it. He used the space under staircase without disturbing any counter. He called it Book-Corner. Soon it became very popular; people took his advice while choosing books. It was the job of his choice and he enjoyed talking with readers. He learned about modern and classic books. When customers asked for a particular book he would arrange it anyhow. He had hardly spent a month here when a cashier left his job. The cashier was a more responsible job. He was asked to take over. His responsibility and labor had increased but his salary had remained same.

Usha visited on his book counter. He suggested her children's book for her elder son who was now three years old. He suggested books of the alphabet and pictures of fruits and animals. She had no money to spend on things like that. The books were of good quality and thus costlier. He gave the books as a gift to her and paid for them. She reminded him to return her money. When he gifted her books she invited him for dinner.

He asked if she had taken permission from her husband. She said she had taken general permission to do anything that she wants to do.

The invitation was in her eyes. He could read it. Anybody who would see them talking could decipher it easily. She was a mother of two and he was a veteran bachelor. Yet the equation was perfect. Or it would remain perfect till he returns her money.

That was one exceptional evening. Bhola did not drink so he had taken two pegs at room before departure, which was just enough to put him on mood. He wore his new dress that he bought at the time of his cousin sister's marriage. He had bought a bottle of perfume from the mall, for such occasion. When he reached Usha was alone. Her children slept in the bedroom. She might have breast fed her younger son, for the lower two buttons of her blouse were open, exposing lower half of her breast. In town women never covered their breast while feeding their children. Breasts were seldom seen as anything erotic. In cities people go crazy by deep necklines. In town every woman would wear a backless blouse and nobody would even notice. The urban people have become perverted due to lot of taboos. What sensuality they could see in breasts which were just mammary glands to feed a child. She tried to push her breast up but could not succeed and ultimately pulled them up by inserting hand from neckline. Then she buttoned her blouse, which had patches of dried milk in the center of cups.

He looked nonchalantly. His mind was somewhere else. One old woman came. She had come to return threads and inform that she would not make crochet net for her anymore. Her payment was overdue and she had to buy medicines for her sick husband. Now she would make paper bags from newspaper. Those people paid cash. He was embarrassed. The old woman had gone but Usha kept on looking at him accusingly. He had adversely affected the life of people. His sin was unforgivable. He would like to compensate, she would not accept anything except money in compensation and he did not have that. If she would ask for anything else he would do. Bhola had come back from the temple in the colony where he went for evening prayers. He could feel the tension between his friend and his wife. Bhola never tried to know anything, unless it was told to him.

Usha's brother came from town to study in high school. He stayed with Bhola and Usha. He could not secure good rank in secondary due to poor English. The boy looked much younger than his age, almost child. He did not like boys who do not grow up to their age. When he was sixteen and most of his friends had a small tuft of hair on chin and a thin line of scattered hair above upper lip he had become nervous about himself. Thankfully his beard and moustaches also appeared within a year's time. He remembered having spent that one year in the anxiety of lack of manhood. There was a group of transgender who appeared at every auspicious occasion of childbirth and marriage to collect gifts and money. If they were not satisfied they would curse which was said to be effective. They would lift their skirts to expose rudimentary genitals and clapped in a queer way and uttered obscenities. Everyone had to satisfy them. He had heard that they picked up those children who lacked gender. He was worried if his moustaches and beard did not grow, not only he would be laughed at by his friends but eunuchs would also hear about him and would pick him up.

Usha requested him to teach English to her brother. He had resolved that he would do anything for her. So he accepted, but he would come at nine in the night with Bhola on a moped and would go his home at ten. Usha contemplated that would leave no time for him to cook, so she offered him to take dinner at her home every night. Such hospitalities were not strange for town people. Food was the minimum courtesy they could offer to an acquaintance of their town any number of times.

It became daily routine for him to go with Bhola to his home on his moped and teach the boy, take dinner and catch last city bus at 10.30.P.M. to reach home and sleep. Every routine howsoever interesting it may look initially loses its charm in the hand of repetition. The boy Sona Ram was a dullard. English for him was a ghost. He was too scared to venture with it.

After teaching Sona Ram for about an hour, he was physically and mentally exhausted. He could not take whisky because from mall he came directly to Bhola's house. Bhola's wife was contended that at least she could recover the interest of money lent by her. She would remind him from time to time that he has to return her money.

When Bhola stayed for overtime he refused to go alone to Bhola's house. Bhola insisted him to go. When he reached Usha was in jovial mood. She asked her brother to study on his own in another room, and take care of children also. She knew how to take full advantage of every situation. Her brother was now a caretaker of her children. Her father paid the expenses as it was a custom never to be a financial burden on daughter. She sat down to gossip with him.

She asked him some questions about bachelorhood and celibacy. The more he shunned, the more she shoved. She asked him about the girl he was betrothed in childhood. He didn't know much about her. She informed him that she was in an Engineering College in the same city and her name was Kiran. Usha was in touch with her, since in primary school they were class fellows. To tease him further she asked for money. Like always he made a false promise to return it at the earliest. She said you must be having money but you don't want to give. With this remark she started searching his pockets. She took out a handkerchief from his pocket which was dirty and she feigned disgust. Then she took out his pocket comb. He resisted her exploration and while doing so he touched her body parts. She inserted her hands in both the pockets of his trouser to deep explore, and while doing so she stood so close to him that there was no gap between them, and her hands manipulated him for some time, before he pushed her away with great force.

She reverted with gusto and fervor. It was unexpected for him. He fell down on the bed by her thrust. Reflexively he had caught her to maintain balance; she also fell down over him. The buttons of her blouse had become loose due to frequent use and her breasts were swollen with milk, so when she fell down over him the buttons were opened and her breast came out. Due to the pressure of his chest the breast was squeezed and a stream of milk dropped in his open mouth. She laughed hysterically and he threw her on one side with all his force. He rushed to spit out the milk but it had already reached to his stomach. While he spat she continued to pass indecent comments with amused laughter.

He was disgusted and called Sona Ram to teach. Usha went into the kitchen and served him food. He checked homework of Sona Ram and then ate the food. He left without any conversation with Usha.

He stopped going to Bhola's house. He made an excuse that he was pursuing graduation privately and would be busy in preparing for exams. This was true, but he had taken this step in retaliation. Consequently when next time Bhola stayed for overtime she dropped at his room. Luckily he was studying a course book. She said he had no right to be annoyed. She had not deliberately forced him to drink her milk. It was just an accident and he should take it in that spirit. If he had returned her money in time this would not have happened. Why she would search his pocket if he had returned her money? There was some logic in her accusation. His ultimate failure to return her money was the cause of all his calamities. His guilt made him humble and he offered her to sit down and offered a glass of water. Usha was pacified.

She appreciated that he had resumed his studies. She said he had a great potential to rise to a high post, if he would study sincerely. She kindled in him a desire to touch the sky. She said he should teach a lesson to Kiran for underestimating him. He told her that he was not interested in Kiran but he wants to do something for his own self. Usha told that if he would meet Kiran he would not say this thing; she was exceptionally beautiful and intelligent girl. This aroused a curiosity in him but he suppressed it. He had accepted her refusal in a spirit without any malice. She had a right to choose her life partner and live with him as she liked.

Usha had brought a big mango for Vicky. She took out a knife from the shelf and cut vertical long pieces. She tasted half and found it sweet, and gave the rest to him. He squeezed the pulp between his teeth and put skin on a plate. To avoid repetition he picked up next slice himself and bit at the half by his teeth when she brought her face closer to his and took remaining half of the slice in her mouth. Both sucked on the pulp from the same slice at the same time. Even when the pulp finished their lips remain locked till they realized that it was not pulp but the lips they were sucking on, and the skin had fallen on the floor long back.

He dislodged himself and went on the balcony with a glass of water to gargle. She wiped her lips with her scarf and threw remaining mango in the dustbin.

Nothing ever happened perfectly with him. He was deprived of female company required in his age, but he was not desperate. He liked Usha but she was the wife of his friend and mother of two children. It would be immoral to be tempted by her provocations. He never knew where the women draw a boundary line. Suppose if he takes a step forward and she withdraws and rebukes him and make a complaint to her husband. He was not prepared to face any humiliation for the sake of any woman's company. He could never understand a woman, they were like silk chocolate wrapped on stones. She might be searching for an excuse to humiliate him. He would not give her that opportunity.

He had a natural talent for literature. His town had a public library. Surprisingly the librarian had a good taste in books. Besides government aid he collected donations from rich people to buy high quality books. The library was famous in the whole district for richness. When he was not with friends he was in the library. His friends had to force him out of it. He found it easy to live in a world of imagination than live in the real world. He could identify his own vacuum with that of the characters in some novels. He was consoled that there are people like him who are not made to live a normal life. Those characters influenced his mind severely and he would live in their company for many days even when he had finished the book. Then he would reread it.

As if that was not enough; he would behave like those characters. His friends called him eccentric but respected him for his knowledge and intelligence. In town he lived in controlled conditions but when he took admission in college hostel he realized multiple dimensions of freedom. In college there was no dress code which was most hateful to him. Most of the lecturers did not take attendance, or they did not mind if somebody else does proxy. The library, cafeteria and swimming pool became his favorite hangouts. When he was in final year he received the news that the parents of the girl he was betrothed with had applied for separation in caste court. She was student of the Engineering College. He had seen her a few times in family functions. She looked beautiful and intelligent. It hurt him. He wanted to meet her and explain he had no objection if she becomes an engineer provided she doesn't mind that he writes the book. Would she understand? He had a doubt. He receded in depression, became melancholic and found solace in drugs.

The daughter of the warden, Anjali was also a student of the same college. She got involved with one of his friends, Raju. They used to meet at the swimming pool, which was his favorite hangout.

Behind swimming pool was a deserted place which was used as a shooting range by NCC. Except Sundays when NCC camps were held, the place was solitary. His best friend Raju called Anjali behind swimming pool. She came with a friend. When Raju and Anjali went behind Bull's eye he was left alone with a friend of Anjali. He was not in any mood for formalities; he directly asked if she wants better experience than her friend is having behind the target. She was smart; she smiled and nodded her head in agreement. He kissed her on the lips and she reciprocated. It was not common to set up an instant affair, the boys usedto spend many weeks before they could steal a kiss of their beloved. We did everything except coitus before Anjali and Raju returned.

Later he told Raju about it, and he was surprised that he had accomplished much more than him. His colleagues saw it as a victory, but he thought what is there to conquest which you can conquest forever. A temporary victory is no victory. Soon they would become just a face in the crowd. Victory is in winning the heart of a girl and then breaking it, she would never forget you especially if you are the first one to do it.

Anjali was ready to elope with Raju. Raju was from his town. His father was a staunch Brahmin. He would never accept a Bishnoi girl. The girls of Bishnoi clan were known to be promiscuous and had different cultural values. A satellite Dhani (hamlet) of his town was inhabited by Bishnois. Some traditions of their culture were secret. The warden was Professor of History. He belonged to a town solely inhabited by people of his clan. His father was a petty criminal. Like all other members of his community they were involved in drug peddling, illicit wine and opium trade. Most of them had been in prison many times. The mother of Professor supplied milk in the house of Vice –Chancellor. They lived in a makeshift hut near the VC house. The VC was a widower and the mother of the warden was fair colored with sharp features and a golden nose ring looked beautiful to VC especially because she came to deliver milk late in the evening when VC had already taken few pegs of whisky. VC invited her inside and offered whisky. He knew Bishnoi women drink liquor to increase sexual appetite. She hesitated but when VC insisted she agreed. No woman could be better than her for a sex hungry VC.

During one of these sessions she took a promise from VC that he would employ her son at the university. Her son was doing a post graduation in the History at that time. VC kept his promise and appointed her son as Lecturer in the department of History when he finished his post graduation.

Dr. Bishnoi father of Anjali caught Raju and Anjali red-handed when they met in the backyard of his bungalow one night. The girl received a thrashing from her mother and Raju was handed over to police on charges of trespass and theft. He went to the warden's house and had heated arguments in support of his friend. Warden knew about his drug habits so he accused him as an accomplice of Raju in police case. Police raided his room and drugs were recovered. They were rusticated from college.

At that time his father was undergoing a financial crisis. He refused to pay for his expenses and he came back to town without finishing his studies. Life was good in town. He had no responsibilities and no burden of studies. He had left his drug habit, town people abhorred drugs. Living was not costly in town. They had their own house. His father was veteran grocer and bought wheat and lentils in the season enough for the whole year. His mother prepared spices at home. They had a good cow, she gave enough milk and butter for the family, buttermilk was given free to anyone who needs. The electric bill was low due to fewer electric gadgets.

His mother spent most of her time watching religious serials on television.

His father opened his shop at fixed hours.

The sale had reduced but his father was not ready to change with the change of time.

His mother did not like his idling. She had already sold most of her jewelry to meet other day to day expenses. She insisted him to go and work in the city. She did not propose him to take over shop because she knew that was the lifeline of her husband.

He never considered any work as menial; everything you do could teach you a lesson provided you are ready to learn.

And that he was.

His exams of final year were approaching closer. He had to fill up examination form and deposit the fees. The fee was eight hundred rupees. If he curtailed his needs he would save three hundred rupees, still he would need five hundred rupees more.

He had started preparing for examination. He cannot afford to waste one year just because of money. Beg Borrow or Steal. First and last solutions were too petty for his ego. So he decided to borrow. When he had mentally surveyed his friends and acquaintances he found all were as hard pressed as him. He had no wealthy friend. He decided to develop friendship with some wealthy person who can help him in need. But why would a wealthy man make him friend? He has no talent which a wealthy man would like to encash.

One of his colleagues salesmen was very popular with rich clients of the Mall. His name was Govind. Rich people would look for Govind if he is not on the counter. Not only that many college girls and educated women also preferred to go on the counter of

Govind, many of them had his mobile number and they would contact him. Floor Manager also kept him in good humor. Govind was also a town boy like him. Then what was so special in Govind. First he would make friends with Govind.

He talked with Bhola about Govind. Bhola was evasive and finally said that he should remain away from Govind. That made him more curious and he started gossiping with Govind in idle time. Govind had seen him talking with the wife of Bhola. After some informal talks Govind asked him about his relationship with Usha. He said there is no relationship she is just a wife of a friend. Govind was sure there was something more than that.

He hanged around Govind's counter when some college girl lingered and tried to eavesdrop. He could judge that Govind had no affair with any one of them. They seemed to be talking business. What business these girls and young women had with Govind. Sometimes they were fixing up a venue and time, obviously not for him because those were the busy hours of the mall. Sometimes he would introduce a girl to floor manager also. Then the floor manager would invite the girl in his cabin for juice or cold drinks. All girls and young women were from middle class families. They were either college students or wives of middle class youth, who came in rickshaw, city bus or by own scooter. Rich people who came to talk with Govind were having posh chauffeured cars. It descended slowly but ultimately he could put two and two together. Govind was a mediator. He provided girls to rich people for entertainment. He was paid commission for this. Rich and middle class both are afraid of society. They would do anything provided their social prestige remained high. The middle class and lower middle class girls were ambitious and had unlimited excuses to spend an afternoon away from home. In their neighborhood they might be quoted as an example of simplicity and sincerity but inside they would laugh for being a whore. Govind would oblige Floor Manager time to time without any charges. It was a highly profitable set up for Govind. There was no investment, no risk and all gain. Rich guys took the girls to five star hotels or to their own farm house which were safe. Govinda was a guarantor from both the sides. Both the parties wanted safety which was ensured by Govind. He had instructed the girls never tell their original name or address to clients, no mobile number, no photos. The girls had blind faith in the command of Govind. His business had spread by mouth publicity only so he saw to it that none of his clients from either the sides is dissatisfied. If there is some minor dispute he would intervene and resolved it. His girls were highly cooperative and rich clients were very generous.

Govind never confessed his involvement in any illicit activities. He always presented himself as hand to mouth. He told that people come to seek his advice on marketing. Govind was taken aback when he denied his relationship with Usha. He knew Usha was prone to temptation and he had made an offer to her, but since her husband worked in the same mall she had declined. Govind thought now she had sent an offer through him, so he had initiated the topic.

He talked with Usha. Usha knew about the nefarious activities of Govind, and also that she was also offered empanelment. Both of us avoided passing any judgment on Govind. Usha agreed that she declined because her husband works in the same mall, and not because she found it morally wrong. For him nothing was moral or immoral. He had simple likes and dislikes. And he disliked what Govind was doing without any specific reasons. What Usha said implied that if the offer comes from some other person she may consider.

The crochet lace is a skilled work. Only a few women knew how to make patterns. It was long and tedious work and comparatively remuneration was low. She started making chain of beads. She engaged about a dozen women from her neighborhood who wanted to work in afternoon to earn few extra bucks. She brought beads, patterns and fish thread from the Mall and made chains as per order. The output of work was fast and payment was better. Usha had just collected her payment from the counter when he remembered that the next day is the last date for depositing exam fees. He went to Usha, who was counting her currency notes and took out one 1000 Rupee note from her hand. She was shocked and furious. Before she could speak anything he left her standing paralyzed. He walked out of the Mall and went to university straight to deposit fee.

Same night Usha came to her room. She told her many heated words standing on the threshold. He invited her inside but she refused. Her nostrils were swollen and lips were trembling. Her cheeks flushed due to anger. Her bosom heaved due to irregular breathing. She even thumped the floor with her feet.

For the first time he found her desirable. He felt excited and evoked. He caught her arms and pulled her in. It was so sudden and unexpected for her that she fell in his arms. He held her tightly and put his own dried lips on her wet quivering lips.

Nobody knows what is the best way to silence a vocal woman? It worked for him, and for the next hour there was no sound except heavy breathing and seldom moans.

He rested flat on the mattress and she sat squat with her arms around her knees hiding most of her nakedness. All her frustration and rage diluted by pent up desires and remorse melted in tears and she started crying. First slowly the tears rolled on her cheeks then she sobbed with a gush of tears.
When she hiccupped her whole body heaved. If she looked pretty in rage, she looked prettier in grief.

A fresh surge of passions overtook him.
He extended his hand to touch her, and she fell down on his body.

Another hour was spent.

He remembered his brief solitary meeting with Usha when they lived in town. There was an empty dried well outside town where Usha took her cattle for grazing. It was said to be cursed and nobody went near it. Once he happened to cross the field and saw Usha is bending at the mouth of well to make the sound of echo. He was on a bicycle. He got down parked his bicycle and went near well. Usha was so engrossed in echo that she did not hear him coming. He also bent down and shouted her name. The echoes of the cry of Usha and her name were mixed up. She looked up at him and laughed. The laugh was also echoed by well. Then she ran away.

Usha also remembered the incident and a smile came on her face. The spirit of empty well had cursed her for rage, passions, grief and joy at the same time.

He was born cursed for emptiness.

He was that empty well which was always inhabited by spirits in turmoil.

If one spirit is liberated after quenching worldly desires another would come and occupy.

No one would leave him alone with his emptiness.

Another spirit haunted for empty well, found him and decided to dwell.

Kiran dropped in with Usha at the mall next day. Usha brought her directly up to him and asked to guess who she was. He had seen her before. He knew her, but she had changed a lot. He said he doesn't know her. The girl looked hurt, and introduced herself. He said he is busy, begged an excuse and left.

Now he knew what he had missed in his life. That girl was an angel. Why would an angel live in a haunted well made for pathetic spirits? It's good that she sought a separation.
Kiran started visiting the mall frequently. She would linger near his counter and would talk to him awkwardly. He was in transition. Usha visited her room at least twice a week. Bhola did more overtime than before. Now she had stopped talking about the refund of her money, instead she started sending messages on mobile. The day she would send a message she would drop in the night. That became a sort of signal of her arrival. Now he would feel sensual by anticipation when he received the message to refund her money.

She would tease him about Kiran to provoke and instigate him to attack on her for brutal sex. That, which can't fill you, makes you more empty. His emptiness became intense after every visit of Usha. She had told lots of good things about him to Kiran. Kiran saw it as a blunder of her life. Her initial euphoria about being an Engineering student had sublimated and she realized that all brilliant people are not necessarily engineer. People with other professions, especially those pursuing management courses, civil service exams, professors in university were more intellectual. Engineers from IIT, were really talented and had superior reputation than other Engineers.A degree of Engineering from ordinary private or government engineering college had no meaning so far as a bright begining of the carrier was concerned.

Kiran found that Vicky (that was nicknam for Vikram) was handsome, intelligent and well behaved. She had never met anyone like him in Engineering College. Moreover he was hers, or could have been hers, if she had not played the fool after her selection in Engineering College. Thankfully both of them were still bachelors.

Kiran asked Vicky if she could have water and he signaled a boy to bring water. He asked in formality if she wanted tea and she requested for a cold drink. The more she met Vicky, the more she was determined to make him her life partner. She would gift him books of renowned authors. Vicky gifted her chocolates. Both were shy of each other. They would think about a lot of things to discuss but remained silent when met. The silence between them was not uneasy.

His transgression with Usha was not yet over. Before departing from an empty well she wanted to suck in all its emptiness and then handover it to Kiran, who may dwell in it for the rest of her life.

The frequency of her message had increased till one day Bhola got free early and reached home to find that Usha had not yet reached. He was worried and came to Vicky's house searching for her. Luckily the door was closed and he shouted Vicky's name from ground floor first then climbed the stairs to reach to Vicky's room on first floor. By that time they were dressed up and when Vicky opened the door Bhola was standing outside about to knock the door. For a moment his expressions changed when he saw his wife was not there. She walked from the balcony into the room. She looked normal and confident. She asked Bhola why he had come here. Bhola had no reply except that he was worried and if she would have told Sona Ram he would not have come here.

Vicky was surprised how she could make her husband feel guilty for her own sin. She rebuked him for disturbing when she was having a nice time with his friend and he was apologizing for being stupid enough to come under anxiety. Every relationship reaches its level of comfort. They went away without any further argument.

Kiran lived in the Girl's Hostel of Engineering College. She was due for summer placement to understand the practical working of the company. She asked Vicky to manage some good company for her summer placement. Vicky talked with Govind. One of his clients was having his office on the upper floor of the mall. The name of his company was Era Electrical. They made heavy-duty cables in the industrial area. Govinda talked with him and he agreed to employ her. Kiran joined in the office on the upper floor of the Mall. The owner of the company was a gentleman and Kiran went with him to the factory to work as Production Manager. Mr. Bansal the owner was impressed by her intelligence and offered her a job after graduation. She said she had not decided whether she would go for higher studies or find a job. If she decides for a job she would gladly join, since she would be able to meet Vicky. She thought.

Now they met daily. Vicky suggested her to read books in spare time. She had no taste for literature. She still liked to read comics. Vicky suggested her few books as a beginner. He said he does not lend his books but as an exception, he would lend her one. She wanted to come to his room, but Vicky refused. He lived in very poor condition in comparison to his life in town. Kiran's father was a landlord in town of high status.

Once when Kiran while going to her office stopped at Vicky's counter. Her father came to meet her in the hostel. He had come to know that she frequently met Vicky. His prestige was at stake in the town. Such rumors spread very fast in small towns. She wanted her parents to be proud of her, but time and again she did things that humiliated her parents in society.

The town was known as Bhadrajun. It was located at the foothills of Aravali range of mountains. Most of the people depended on agriculture for livelihood. The town was dominated by Bishnoi and Rajput community. Vicky was from the business community but all his friends were Rajput. Though his family was strictly vegetarian but he in parties would drink and eat meat. That's why when Kiran refused to marry him, her father did not oppose her. Now he heard that his daughter was seen by Vicky in the mall disturbed him. He had come to know that Usha is also in touch with Vicky. Being a man of high reputation in the town he always looked down upon the people of lower community. In his opinion they deserved to be exploited in all possible ways. The mother of Usha used to work in his fields. She was also good-looking like her daughter. He would call her for a massage in his rest rooms made on tube well in the field. The girls of lower community took it granted that it is their duty to appease the people of a higher community. Sometimes Usha also went to help her mother in the fields. When she could not find her mother one afternoon she went up to the rooms near tube-well. She saw her mother in compromising position with the father of her friend Kiran. She could recognize him even from his back. Her eyes met with her mother and she asked her to go away. Her mother was scared that if he would see her daughter he may demand her. In town many rich people of the upper community had relation with mother and daughter both.

Usha had returned that day but her desires had inflamed. Her eyes were always searching for a suitable boy. She did not like the boys of her own community. Neither they could give her a costly gift, nor did they drink costly wine and wear clothes like boys of the upper community.

Once when she took the cattle for grazing near empty well and made a sound to hear the echo a cat jumped out from dried well who was hiding under the stone of boundary wall of the well. The cat jumped suddenly on her face and she fainted. While falling on the ground she saw a young man was running towards her. That was Mohan Singh.

When she came back to senses she realized that she was naked and Mohan Singh was rubbing briskly on her whole body. He was holding her in his hands and from time to time gave her mouth to mouth breathing. She realized that her whole body which had gone cold by fear of cat had regained normal breathing and temperature. Mohan Singh did not stop his hands or mouth and soon her body was hot by rush of blood. She had no desire to resist what her body hungered for.

It was summer afternoon. The place was totally deserted. The silence was broken by the occasional bleat of goats. There was a tree near well, Mohan had brought her under tree to save from the sun. There were bushes in the shadow of the tree. Mohan had a water bottle with him. He washed her face and poured some water in her mouth, while she was still lying on the ground. Mohan had come to know that it was her first time and was glad to take her care.

While lying under a tree, she looked up and saw that cat was sitting on a branch of the tree and was staring at her. The cat must have watched her making love also. Usha screamed and held Mohan tightly, closed her eyes and hid her face in the tuft of hair on the chest of Mohan. Mohan saw the cat and picked up a stone to throw at her, but before Mohan could throw his stone she jumped and disappeared in the bushes. Usha was still shivering, while he held her naked body tightly. Mohan believed that a second round is always better than the first round.

The empty haunted well became a clandestine rendezvous for Usha and Mohan. The place was safe, due to its defamation as haunted. Mohan would always bring some gifts for her. So far she had eaten candies from her pocket- money; Mohan introduced her to the world of chocolates. He gifted her hair clips, ribbons, bangles, talcum powder, lipstick and lots of other similar things which town girls always fancied. Mohan Singh was a Rajput and liquor was part of his life. He would bring cans of beer and omelets to celebrate the ritual. On such occasion Usha would throw her packed lunch of two thick chapatis, piece of pickle and onion in the dried well.

She would say "This is for the spirits to keep me happy." She thought what her body enjoyed was her happiness.

Once a Bishnoi boy became suspicious and followed Mohan from a distance. Usha was grazing her cattle. When she saw Mohan, she went under the tree. Mohan Singh reached after five minutes. The name of Bishnoi boy was Dhara Ram. He could deduce what was going on between Mohan and Usha. Girls having illicit affairs were considered as public property for felonious vagabonds. Dhara conveyed this news to friends of his group. The group was hilarious to learn it. When they would celebrate the victory, Dhara would be given first chance as per rules.

The leader of the gang of bishnois was, Bheeka Ram. He was well built and muscular man who spent many hours every day doing exercises to keep his body fit. His cousin brother was in the police force and he had influence in political parties also. Bheeka Ram made a plan and asked them to execute when Mohan Singh is away from town. After a week they came to know Mohan had to take his grandfather to Hardwar for a dip in the holy Ganges. When the gang was sure that Mohan had left for Hardwar for four days, they decided to execute the plan on the second day of his departure.

One Bishnoi boy who looked comparatively innocent went in the grazing field. He approached to Usha from the side of the grove where a pond was inhabited by a cobra. He told her that one of her goats had strayed and was attacked by a cobra near pond. The girl ran towards the pond without counting her goats. In town people trust generally while in cities people doubt first.

The gang was already waiting, Usha could know that she was trapped and started yelling and pleading. When it didn't work she threatened to complaint to Sarpanch and Mohan Singh. The boys were in the habit of receiving pleadings and threatening. They gagged her and had their own way. They would never injure the girl, not even a scratch. They would rather try to please her and plead her to enjoy the act. They would also explain that there is no difference between them and Mohan. They don't have spikes on their organ and that she would forget Mohan once they administer it into her.

The Bishnoi gang left after each member had his multiple rounds. Usha was lying on the ground with open legs and cramps in the lower abdomen. She was thirsty, and her throat choked but she had no strength left to get up, and go near water. Her clothes were neatly piled on a rock nearby. Her body and mind had gone numb and she was unable to feel or think anything except shame and humiliation. A brown empty cocoon fell from the tree under which she was lying. She decided to keep it as a souvenir.

When Mohan Singh came back, Usha told him the entire episode. He lost his temperament, and decided to teach the gang of Bishnois a lesson. When he talked with his friends, they reminded him that a few months back one Rajput boy had eloped with the minor Bishnoi girl and head of both the clans met to settle the issue without police intervention.

When Mohan Singh asked the father of Usha to file a complaint in the Police, he flatly refused. Already he had found a boy who was ready to marry Usha. He denied the occurrence of any such incident. Mohan Singh insisted, so both the gangs had a face to face meeting. Bheeka Ram openly admitted his act, but challenged Mohan Singh to prove his cause of concern. He said he would apologize only if Mohan Singh intended to marry the girl. It was a valid objection, since in town it was not possible to monopolize the girls of lower community for enjoyment by any one person.

Ultimately Rajput gang withdrew without any action. Mohan Singh stopped meeting Usha who was now engaged to a man of her own community. Bhola Ram was happy that his wife was beautiful. He tried to meet her before marriage but Usha refused. He inferred that rumors about the character of Usha were baseless. She was decent, a homely girl with good moral values.

Next time when Usha came to Vicky's room she was upset. She had a tussle with her husband. Bhola Ram had full faith in the prudence of his wife but he did not like his wife accepting money from her parents for taking care of her younger brother. Her parents were poor but they had self- respect. They did not want to increase the financial burden of their daughter. So they paid a token amount of two hundred rupees per month for lodging and boarding of Sona Ram. They bore expenses on school fees and books also. Her mother would also send vegetables, pure butter oil, millets and spices whenever possible. Usha was indirectly reminding him that he owes her fifteen hundred rupees. Vicky remained silent. He did not like the topic of money. He was more interested to know about Kiran. He did not pay much attention to the rant of Usha. Usha could feel that he was avoiding the topic of money and she was frustrated. When she could not do charity to her own brother, why does he expect her to be benevolent to him? Mohan Singh was better than him; at least he gave her many gifts and kept her in good humor. So when Vicky asked her why Kiran did not attend her marriage, she blurted out that Kiran was a whore and she had an abortion in city hospital when Usha was getting married to Bhola Ram.

Vicky was thunderstruck. He presumed that Usha was harsh due to her frustration. He looked hard at Usha to correct her statement. Usha stared back at him bluntly. At that moment Vicky became sure that what Usha was saying was true. He was speechless. Then he asked who he was, and Usha said Mohan Singh. He had a severe nausea and went on the balcony to vomit. Nothing came out except yellow-green bile. He took a bottle of water and gargled to clear his throat from the bitter taste of bile and its pungent smell. Usha came and rubbed his back. Vicky stopped her. He did not want any sympathy. He wanted to be left alone, but couldn't ask Usha to go. The truth chooses its own moment to be revealed. Vicky couldn't walk properly and Usha had to support him back to the mattress where he rested lifeless with eyes closed when Usha left his room silently.

Vicky went to the city hospital in the morning. He remembered the date of marriage of Bhola. One of his class fellows from college worked in the hospital ministerial staff. He asked for his help. Soon the record of Obstetrics ward was before him. Kiran had remained in the hospital for a week for treatment of severe bleeding followed by the abortion. On the record, the name of her husband was Vikram, which was the original name of Vicky. Her parents had brought her and they had signed her discharge papers.

Mohan Singh had spoiled two women he had loved so far in his life. But there was no fault of Mohan in it; both had fallen for Mohan on their own. Mohan never said No to a willing girl, in his dictionary it was a sin to refuse any willing girl. Vicky had no remorse against Mohan. Nor he had any grudge against Usha or Kiran. Mohan was so handsome and rich that every girl in town was crazy for him. It was a matter of chance that Mohan was the first lover of both the girls he loved.

Vicky came back to his room and informed his floor manager that he would not be coming as he was sick. He had brought a bottle of whiskey while returning from hospital. It was the peak of summer but suddenly dense clouds covered the sky, and it started raining. The rain intensified the grief of Vicky and he settled on the balcony in the rain with the bottle of whisky. The gulp of neat whisky drew a line of fire up to his stomach.

When Vicky did not reach the Mall, Bhola was worried and he informed Usha to go and check if Vicky was in need of some help. Usha reached Vicky's room in the afternoon holding an umbrella and partly soaked by torrential rain she found that Vicky was lying on the balcony totally drunk and senseless. She was also soaked while she dragged him inside the room. She took off all his clothes and rubbed him vigorously with dry towel. She wrapped him in a bed cover. Then she opened all her clothes and dried her body. She squeezed away all water from her clothes and hanged them on a thin plastic rope. She wore a jeans and T-shirt of Vicky. She untied her braid and dried her hair with a towel. Her hairs were black long and lustrous. Few free-floating locks loomed on her cheeks enhancing her beauty. She saw herself in the mirror and was shy and proud of her beauty.

Vicky squirmed on the bed. Usha came closer and put her palm on his cheeks. Vicky blinked his eyes a few times to make it sure that he was alive and with a beautiful woman or he was dead and in heaven with an Apsara. Usha was wearing his clothes. The T-shirt was tight on her heavy bosom and the tits jutted against the coarse cotton clothes of his T- shirt. The jeans were tight on the thighs accentuating her figure. She prepared tea for him. She had made all the preparation to cook food.

When he finished tea, she fumbled in her bag and took out a plastic case used for keeping jewelry by women. She opened and took out an empty cocoon and gave it to him. He looked inside the empty cocoon. It reminded him of the empty well where he had met Usha for the first time. Why does she carry an empty cocoon with her? She said it is the gift for him. Then she told him the entire story of her relationship with Mohan Singh and her subsequent rape by half a dozen Bishnoi gang.

Now he knew why she gave him the empty cocoon that she had carried since her rape in the grove. Her life had become empty after that incident. She could not see any relationship objectively. Her entire existence had become hollow like a shell of the cocoon and the emptiness within was greater than emptiness all around it.

Now that cocoon with all its emptiness was in his palm. He delicately puts it back in plastic case. It was a symbol of all the truth that were revealed to him since yesterday. Truth leads to emptiness and absolute truth to absolute emptiness.

Bishnoi is a clan originated in the deserts of Rajasthan. They are known for fanatic belief in protection of nature and wildlife. The community is also prone to misdemeanor offenses like illegal distilling of alcohol and smuggling opium for local consumption. The youth of clan is also united and dedicated for twenty nine tenets coined by the founder.

Bheeka Ram was the leader of a group of half a dozen like minded youth of the Bishnoi clan in Bhadrajun town. His group maintained the balance of power with Rajput youth who would otherwise not pay the minimum wages to the labor of other communities that worked in their field.

Three years back when Kiran was in final year of school, one Bishnoi boy fell in love with her. He would chase her when she went to school and returned home. He would pass remarks at her, and would sing obscene songs. Once he stopped her on the way and thrust a love letter in her hand. She was constantly pestered and felt frustrated and decided to take some action. The school authorities had failed time and again in providing protection to female students from vagabonds. Her father was very strict and the first thing he would do, was withdrawing her from school. She wanted to make a career in the field of engineering. One of her friends suggested contacting Mohan Singh. She had no idea who Mohan Singh was? She was totally dedicated to studying. Her friend Kirti Singh was also Rajput and Mohan Singh was her cousin. She called Mohan Singh outside school and introduced Kiran to him. Kiran told him how she was harassed by a Bishnoi young man. Mohan Singh said he would take care. The next day when she was on her way to school she saw that Mohan had stopped the young man from stalking her. She did not even look at them. After that day she was never bothered by that young man again. She thanked Kirti and sent a thank you card to Mohan. Mohan reverted with chocolates and a yellow rose.

After her senior secondary exams Kiran went to the city for coaching. She took the entrance test of Engineering College, and came back to town awaiting result. The town of Bhadrajun has been just outside the railway station on one side. The other side had few railway bungalows only. The town spread in the radius of two kilometers. Haat was a weekly market held in the central row of town on every Wednesday when folklore of nearby towns brought agriculture produces, handmade tools and woodcraft to sell. Tribes bought and sold commodities by barter system as well as on cash payment. By the end of the day they would buy things that they could not produce in towns like, salt and clothes. There were about fifty houses of upper communities in the town mostly around the haat. The people of lower community who did menial jobs of labor on farms lived outside the town. Some of them were barbers, iron-smith, shoemakers etc. The lowest communities were untouchables who were either sweepers or those who removed hide from a carcass.

Usha was from meghwal community and her parents worked in the field as labors. They were also involved in weaving pattu a woolen shawl or small carpets called durry. These goods were in demand in metropolitan cities and by exporters. The artisans of lower communities earned bare minimum wages. The middleman earned the real profit. Even then the weavers community was happy, since rainfall was not consistent and they had alternative means of survival in case of famines.

The houses of lower caste were on the periphery of the town on the other side of the pond. The untouchables lived at the farthest end. Around central haat was the magnificent house of Kiran's father. Behind it was their huge orchard of best Mango trees in the entire zone of towns that produced Mangoes. The house of Kiran had a high boundary wall and one small gate opened in the back orchard. Any grownup would have to bend double to go through it. Kiran's mother was illiterate but intelligent lady who took good care of the family. She favored higher education for Kiran against the wishes of her husband. She did not support her daughter in seeking divorce from Vicky. Her gut feeling was that Vicky was a nice boy and he would keep her daughter happy. In her opinion that is what ultimately mattered.

Kiran had come back to town after taking her entrance exam. She was sure about her success. She spent her leisure on romantic novels. Her mother never asked her to help in domestic chorus. During summer vacation her friend Kirti who was not allowed to go to the city for higher education came to visit her. They sat in the privacy of Kiran's room. Kirti was betrothed to a smart Rajput young man of a nearby town. His name was Sunder. He was popular as Sunder Banna. She talked with him every day on mobile and the young man was crazy after her. He sent Kirti erotic messages on mobile and Kirti read them to Kiran. Kiran was shocked by such frank and bold comments and felt shy also. Kirti had told Sunder that she read all his comments to her friend

Kiran. Kiran was more fair and looked delicate while Kirti had strong bones and looked mature. Sunder was also a friend of Mohan Singh.

Sunder sent message to Kirti that his friend Mohan is madly in love with Kiran. He sent messages on behalf of Mohan Singh for Kiran and asked Kirti to reply. Kirti asked Kiran if she likes Mohan.

It was summer when days are lengthier and monotonous. The afternoons are spent in siesta and smoking hookah by elderly persons and children play near pond under the shadow of trees. The young men go to the city every day to watch movies and kill the time loitering in gardens or with their friends who were doing business or higher studies in the city. The young men doing higher studies stayed in the city to prepare for competitive examination. The young girls are confined to the premises of their house and were left to boredom.

On such a hot afternoon when the entire town was in the grip of awkward silence, Kiran and Kirti were idling under a Mango tree in the orchard where they had come to taste ripened Mangoes. Kirti read the latest message of Sunder on mobile sending hugs and kisses for her. In the last he wrote that his friend Mohan is eagerly waiting for the reply of her friend and has stopped eating and sleeping. Kirti looked at her when she finished reading the message. In her heart she knew the reply of her friend. It is then Kiran Said, Tell him I too love Mohan. Kirti was awestruck by the confession of her friend. She looked at her quizzically. Kiran looked at the tree as if searching for ripened Mango, but her face was dark pink and eyes shined in excitement when she looked in the eyes of her friend and repeated that she loved Mohan since the first day she met him. Kirti jumped out of joy and embraced her friend.

Kiran did not have mobile at that time though Mohan had one. Mohan wanted to gift her one set but she could not accept. Mohan sent messages for Kiran on the mobile set of Kirti when she was with her every afternoon. The fire was inflamed everyday to a new height and both the girls burned in the fire of passions. Mohan and Sunder were insisting to meet them which both the girls avoided since in their heart they knew the consequences.

Once the sister of Sunder came to meet her Sister-in Law Kirti, she brought sweets, dresses and fruits for Kirti. When alone she gave a CD to her and asked her to watch it secretly. Kirti brought that CD to Kiran, since she did not have a computer. They bolted the room to watch what it was? It turned out to be a porn movie of two couples. They were aroused and same day sent a consent to meet them.

At the farthest corner of the Mango orchard was a tube well and one room was built for guard. The room was empty since guard lived in his own house in the town and he came only at night. The trees were dense and nothing was visible from outside the fence even in day time. They decided to meet at 2.00 PM in the afternoon at tube well. It seemed like luck favored the lovers. No hindrance happened and all the four reached near tube well with their hearts beating like muffled drums. The initial shyness and hesitation was soon taken over by overwhelming passions and it is here both the girls lost their virginity.

A cuckoo was singing melodious song and air ruffled the young twigs of Mango tree when both the girls lay exhausted amongst the dried Mango tree leaves. A ripened Mango fell from tree between both the couples still entwined with each other. All the four sucked on that Mango for some time, one after another to seal their bonding.

The affair continued for quite some time. They met at every opportunity, even at midnight, when the guard was on leave or fast asleep. The danger made the expeditions more romantic. All the four of them were now devoid of any shame and even joked about swapping. Kiran had a curvaceous delicate body. While making love with his fiancée Sunder imagined about Kiran. He asked Mohan to convince Kiran for him. Mohan had fully exploited Kiran, and he valued his friendship more than his relations with an infatuated girl, so he agreed to talk to Kiran about it.

The parents of Kirti knew Kiran very well and had a high opinion about her. When Kirti went to her house almost every afternoon they did not object. They knew Kiran had no brother and her father spent the whole day on shop so Kiran and her mother were alone in the house in the afternoon. Kiran's mother saw the girls were behaving strangely but she had full faith in her daughter. Whenever she checked suddenly they were gossiping intimately. Then she would go for a siesta and girls would slip through the backdoor into the orchard. Mohan and Sunder were either waiting for them or they would come promptly.

They didn't waste time in talking; they would embrace and kiss and would make love under a dense Mango tree surrounded by shrubs. Sunder had involved his fiancée in the conspiracy. When he talked with her on a mobile phone he expressed his desire to have fun with her friend Kiran. Kirti was shocked but Sunder convinced her that Mohan would never marry with her and when Mohan could enjoy why he should be deprived of that fun. Kirti knew that her friend co-operated more than her during the act and had a beautiful body, she agreed to help sunder in his planning.

The Rajput girls are more open mind than girls of any other caste. Rajput is a warrior clan and they fought battles in ancient time.

One of the best battalions of the Indian army is Rajput Regiment. The Moughals and British also employed Rajput in military force. The chivalry of Rajput was a legend in folklore. They are robust with broad chest and shoulder, and courageous. They eat Non-Vegetarian food and drink alcohol. They keep concubines and the domestic female helpers are also used for sexual gratification. The children born by domestic help are given a status of Half-Rajput called Gola. Even such bastard children had an acceptance and respect in society.

This Rajput had high self-esteem and would do anything to protect the name of family. Since the father of a daughter is considered inferior to the father of a son, they killed their daughters just after birth. The midwife was given instructions that she should put a sand pillow on the face if a female child is born, and kill her by suffocation. The mother was told that a dead baby is born. The girl child was also a risk for reputation. She may fall in love with a boy of other caste and could defame the family. A Rajput father would not hesitate in killing his daughter and his paramour if she falls in love before marriage. Such killings were known as "Honor Killing" and society approved and respected it.

Warriors have a tendency to enjoy the life, they know how momentarily and perishable it is. They spend money on luxuries and entertainment. The Rajput women are also known for bravery. They would sacrifice their life in the funeral pyre of their husband if he died in war. Thousand of Rajput women would enter the huge funeral pyre alive when they heard that their husbands have died in war and enemy force is coming to capture the fort.

Kirti was not surprised by demands of her fiancée. Kiran was a beautiful girl and her contours were well placed. Kirti was fair colored but she had strong bones like her mother. Kiran looked like a model or film actress. Kirti knew neither Mohan nor Sunder would ever marry Kiran. Her wedlock was safe. Such was the tradition of their families. Out of this security, she agreed to help Sunder in acquiring Kiran. She knew her husband would respect her more if she could cajole Kiran for him.

In her heart she was jealous of Kiran. She was more beautiful, intelligent and wealthy than her. She would be happy to see her being treated like a two penny whore. Mohan treated Kiran roughly during the act while her fiancée was gentle, rather almost formal. If given a chance Sunder would be fiercer than Mohan, she was sure about it. He would settle scores for her. She saw no reason why she should not support her fiancé in his endeavor.

Mohan liked Kiran but he did not love her. He liked all beautiful girls for that matter, especially if they were of other caste and hard to conquer. Kiran was not his in the list of "to-do" girls. She had fallen in his lap like a pleasant surprise. He was thankful to Kirti for enticing her. He never spent too much time for one girl. He had had his fill and now wanted to terminate or suspend relation with Kiran so that he can take up other projects. If other girls concluded that he was serious about Kiran his market value would go down. So when Sunder demanded Kiran from him, he was rather pleased and eager to help him.

Now all the four of them stood under Mango tree. Kiran had many bad omens since morning. Her right eyelid fluttered and some neighbor sneezed when she was leaving from the back door. Her heart was still trembling when she reached under the tree. As usual Mohan pulled her towards him with force and her protruding breasts were crushed to his chest. Sunder was still holding the hand of Kirti and she whispered in the ears of Sunder. Sunder looked disappointed and disheartened. When Mohan asked, he told him that Kirti is under period and she would not be available for a week. Then again Kirti whispered standing on her toes and putting her palm across her mouth to make sure she is not overheard. Sunder shook his head and said she should ask her friend. Mohan asked again and Sunder told that Kirti has suggested that he could use her friend if he like her.

It was not unusual amongst them to joke about such offers, so Kiran did not take it seriously. Suddenly Mohan pushed her towards Sunder with a thrust. Kirti stood aside when she saw Kiran wobbled towards him. Sunder took a step forward and took Kiran in his arms. Kiran caught him for balance. Sunder took it as green signal and embraced and kissed on the lips. Kiran could not believe this was really happening to her. Sunder was stronger than Mohan. his grip was tight and she felt like a fish out of water. Kirti was laughing as if it was a big joke. She pulled her Salwar down before Kiran could anticipate her move. Mohan and Kirti stood like onlooker when she was brutally taken by Sunder. Kirti gave her clothes and tried to wipe her tears and straighten her hair afterwards, but Kiran abused and pushed her away.

They went away and exited through a secret hole in the fence from which they came every day. Kiran never met any of them after that incident. She felt ashamed of herself. She was terrified when she missed her periods and felt morning sickness. She knew that it would bring a curse on the whole family. She considered committing suicide. She tried to hang herself by a fan but she fell down from the stool. Her mother heard the noise and came. She saw a stall hanging from the fan and presumed what her daughter was up to. The grief took over Kiran when her mother embraced her. She cried and wailed in the lap of her mother for a long time. Her mother stroked her hair and back affectionately. Then she softly asked who the boy was. Kiran told her the whole story.

Her mother rebuked her for falling for a notorious Rajput boy. She assured Kiran that she would take care and Kiran should keep her lips tightly closed. She consulted the family midwife who was a trusted woman. She suggested some herbal medicines.

Kiran suffered severe bleeding when she took boiled juices of many herbs put together. She had to be taken to the city hospital. To avoid any embarrassment, her mother mentioned Kiran as married to Vikram.

Kiran refused to marry Vicky because she knew she was not worthy of him. She had lost her pride and self-respect after that sad incident. She would tell her story if some boy wants to marry her. She was sure no boy would marry her once he knew truth of her life. This would relieve her from the burden of marriage. She was mentally prepared to live her life alone; though she was sure, her mother would never agree to this. She did not want to increase the agony of her mother, so she would say yes to any proposal that her mother would bring.

She told the entire story to Vicky in the Public garden where they sat on a wooden bench under a Neem tree. Her voice was hollow, devoid of any emotion. Vicky remembered the empty cocoon lying on his shelf. Am I that cocoon? Or Kiran is that cocoon? He knew he had been living a hollow life but Kiran was an embodiment of hollowness. As if a vessel made to contain nectar goes hollow, when a devil drinks the nectar and throws the vessel.

Vicky lost his voice. He had no words of consolation for her. Nothing could console her. Not even a compassionate touch. No Reiki could restore her imbalance. Her poor soul is set to torment for the rest of her life. Her eyes had dried and she had no tears left to lament. Her uterus was damaged and she would never be a mother again. No miracle can cure her emptiness. Vicky was thankful for she confided in him.

When silence was unendurable, he looked at her and passed a weak smile.
She was feeling light and tried to reciprocate.

Every time she thought about the incident, the trauma became alive. She had been raped thousand times in her mind, making her emptier every time.

Vikram was amazed how the caste system determined the psyche of people. Families of Bedia community, which followed the tradition of prostitution, inhabited a neighbor town "Bandar Sindri" on national highway. The girls of every family in that village are prostitutes irrespective of her age. Once married they are no more allowed to continue the profession of cottage industry of sex. Vicky visited that village with his friends out of curiosity. They were afraid of venereal diseases and AIDS, which is of common occurrence in the girls of that village, so they avoided sex with them. He saw that many girls wearing enchanting dresses and heavy make-up made vulgar gesture to invite customers. Some of them were minors. Such young women, at the age when they should be in schools and playgrounds, were in one of the most heinous professions of the world.

Some young girls of this community have shifted to Big cities and work as Bar girls. They wore jeans and kept mobile phones. They did not sell cheap. While other girls remained in the village for safety and felt contended. All males of the village were pimps. They protected their "shops" from scoundrels and Police. They knew how to tackle the customers and save the girls from any hassle. Just because these girls were born in the family of certain caste, they were subjected to live inhumane life.

Kirti accepted that her husband would keep concubines and she did not expect any chastity from him. She valued the unreasonable desire of her husband more than the friendship. Such was the influence of caste on the psyche of the people. Every caste and sub caste had its own value system that has remained part of culture for many centuries and every Indian receives it in inheritance.

Kiran was from business class family. Her caste was of landowners, traders and moneylenders. Laxmi the Goddess of wealth was their Mother-Goddess. They were most wealthy people in the town and believed in multiplication and conservation of wealth. The people of this caste are timid, ate simple healthy food and saw their wives and daughters as an incarnation of Laxmi. They spent part of their income on jewelry for financial security, which kept their wives happy.

Acute boredom and erotic talks between Kirti and her fiancé dragged her into sin, which was simply unpardonable in her family. Her father would have beaten her until half dead and would have married her to any boy of his community even if he were illiterate and poor. Her mother stood like a rock beside her to advocate higher education. Now she was in engineering college, lived in a hostel and met her ex-fiancé frequently. She did not attend the marriage of Sunder and Kirti as she had lost faith in the concept of friendship.

Vikram looked in the eyes of Kiran. He saw the horizon of deserts in her eyes. On the hill near his town was a temple of Hanuman. He went there every Tuesday and Saturday with garland, sweets, coconut and incense to pay homage. On the other side of the hill was a long span of desert. The view of sunset from the hill was mesmerizing. He would sit for hours and stare at the horizon to see the sun setting and then darkness would slowly engulf him. All those sunset left him empty like a cocoon hanged in a vacuum. He saw the same horizon in the eyes of Kiran which touches the mind like a spark and make it blank. They looked at each other with blank eyes and could listen to the wailing of wounded souls of each other. The bells of the temple in the garden chimed for evening prayer and talisman was dispelled.

In the hometown of Vicky an ancient temple of Lord Krishna was located in the center of town. The haat was held in the open space in front of the temple. The temple had mythological significance. It is said that the name of the town Bhadrajun comes from Subhdra and Arjun of great Indian epic Mahabharat. Subhdra was the sister of Lord Krishna who was a friend of Arjuna, the most cherished brother amongst Pandavas. Krishna helped her in eloping with Arjuna and solemnized their marriage in the town of Bhadrajun. The priest was given a conch shell by Arjuna and to the wife of priest Subhdra gave her earrings.

The people of the town were proud of their lineage, especially the priest families were a descendant of the priest who conducted the marriage of sister of Lord Krishna. The Brahmins are most revered caste in Hindu society. They spent their whole life in pursuit of knowledge. They received alms from business class and were protected from enemies by the Rajputs. They lived simple honest life, and performed sacrifices for business class and the Rajputs on all occasions in lieu of donations. All Hindus undergo sixteen sanskararight from the birth till the death. 1. Conceivement of virtuous child by a married couple, 2 &3. In 3,4,6, and 8 months of pregnancy a ceremony for proper development of the fetus, 4. Welcome note to the birth of a child, 5. Sun sight by mother and name ceremony of the newborn child, 6. After four months of birth, the child is taken out of home for the first time, mostly to a temple, 7. After 6 month child is given food of milk and rice, 8. When 1 or 3 years old the hair is cut and head is clean shaved, 9. In 3,5 or 7 years the ears are pierced, 10. In 5 year child is sent to school, 11. The sacred thread ceremony is also called second birth, when adolescents are ready for higher education, 12. Learning Vedas, 13. During his higher education, he did not cut nails and hair, after completion of education he shaves and turns into a gentleman from scholar, 14. Welcome to domestic life by parents, 15.Marriage ceremony with the object to produce a child and get rid of sins of 21 generations, 10 of the past, 10 future and one present generation, 16. Death ceremony when the dead body is offered to one of the five elements, mostly

Fire, and bones of skull are cracked by son by a stick when the body is almost half burnt, to liberate the soul of his father from his body.

On each occasion, Priest performs the rituals and people donate according to their capacity. There were no fixed fees, the gap, in the donation he received from rich and poor was wide, but his quality of performance remained same. The Brahmin girls are most beautiful, intelligent and innocent. Due to indifference for money, they are deeply cultured and value art and literature. Most of them have read ancient Indian scriptures in Sanskrit when they are teenagers. They imbibed the values inculcated in Ramayana for idealism. Most of them visit to a temple every day. The daughter of priest usually takes care of *Sanctum Sanctorum* of the temple.

It is in that temple Vikram saw Megha for the first time. She was the daughter of the priest, and was brought up in the city by her maternal grandparents.

Megha looked different from other town girls. She looked intellectual type of girl without any distortion in her beauty which intelligence usually causes. Vicky went to the temple after a bath for daily rituals. Instead of the priest, his daughter, Megha stood in the sanctum accepting offerings people brought for the deity. Vicky was rusticated from college and had come back from the city in search of solace. His heart missed a beat when he looked at Megha. He stood like statute and forgot to recite his daily prayer. The girl took garland, incense sticks from his hand, and offered them to the deity.

He came to senses by her touch, and started reciting his daily prayer "One thousand names of Vishnu". When he had finished, the girl told him that his pronunciations are incorrect and it would be better if he learned some Hindi prayer. Vikram was taken aback; everyone in the town appreciated his command over Sanskrit prayers. He stared at the girl and she pronounced the first verse of the prayer in Sanskrit. Vikram could know that not only her voice was melodious but also her pronunciation was accurate. Vikram felt insulted and after temple, he went to meet his friends as usual. They told him that her name was Megha and that she was student of university with Sanskrit as special paper and English Literature as minor. Therefore, she was the girl who knew Kalidas and Shakespeare both. Vicky never saw her again in the temple or anywhere else. She remained at home and pursued her studies even during vacations.

He was in search of some excuse to visit her home when one day his mother asked him to deliver a bag of rice to the house of the priest. He chose a time when the priest would be in the temple. He recited one thousand names of Vishnu on his way to please the God, to have an encounter with the girl. God heard his prayers. When he knocked at the door of the house of the priest, the girl opened the door. He stood frozen and could not speak a single word. The girl saw the bag of rice and extended her hand to accept it. Meanwhile her mother came from inside and welcomed Vicky. She asked Megha to bring a glass of water but he refused and though he had come with a plan to linger as long as possible, now he wanted to run away. He touched the feet of wife of the Priest and left in a hurry.

Vicky realised that beauty of the girl made him nervous. The girl observed it and enjoyed his nervousness. She had heard that Vikram was well read and he had a collection of books of the famous authors and noble laureates. She wanted him to stay so that she can seek his guidance for selection of the books to read. However, he ran away as if he had seen a ghost. She could not believe that this young innocent man was rusticated from college for inappropriate behavior.

On the way to the Hanuman temple on the hill, a diversion went up to a cave. Outside the cave, a big flat rock was placed on two boulders, which made a porch outside the cave. From the porch, the view of the town looked very nice. This place was also associated with The Mahabharata and Pandava had spent some time here during exile. The place was called Bheem Bhadak, since Bheem had placed the flat rock outside the cave to make terrace.

Whenever Vicky was in sultry mood, he would go to the cave and the desolate cave would be his cocoon where he would feel as safe as in the womb of the mother. After some time, he would come out of somberness, fresh and light and would stand on the terrace. The town looked like a small patch of red rooftops surrounded by plush green fields of crops.

When Vicky could not talk with Megha, he felt ashamed of himself. He was in his sultry mood and his mother knew she should not pursue him for anything. She would serve him food, but if he did not eat, she would remove the plates. She would not ask him to take a bath or go to temple. He would sleep until afternoon but she would not wake him up. She would serve him tea whenever he woke up. He never refused a cup of tea.

It was the third day since he met with Megha. It was noon and he was still asleep. He had not shaved or combed hair in last three days. He had hardly eaten any meals. He had pulled a cover up to his face, when he heard the same melodious voice that had recited Vishnu mantra to him. He could not dare to uncover his face. Suppose it is not true and he had just imagined her voice. If it is a dream he would prefer to die and make the dream eternal. If it is true he would die of happiness. In either case, it is better for him to lie still. He heard the voice of his mother. She told the girl that Vicky was sleeping and did not like to be disturbed. A silence scared Vicky. He pulled away his cover and saw that girl was examining his shelf of books. Her mother stood helpless since he had given strict instructions that nobody should touch his books without his permission. The girl looked at the books from a distance. She did not see Vicky waking up. When she turned to leave, she saw Vicky sitting on his cot. He looked pale and sick. She had not come to inquire about his health, so she asked if she could borrow a book from him.

He permitted her to choose but she wanted him to suggest. He had to get up. He wore sandoz vest and knickers. Therefore, he begged excuse and went to attached washroom to change his clothes. When he came out, he was wearing an Adidas Tracksuit.

Megha was looking at the back cover of the Albert Camus' book "The Stranger". She asked his opinion and he said it was necessary for any student of English Literature to read it. He said he gave only one book at a time and that too with lots of instructions. Do not dog-ear the page, use a bookmark, do not underline the favorite sentences, do not sublet the book, and do not read while eating food lest it may spoil the book. The girl laughed, her white teeth glittered and music was amazing. He asked why she laughed, and she told that she also gives the same instructions when she lends a book.

She said she was a voracious reader and would finish the book in a day . Mother intervened and said she could come whenever she wished. Then she went into the kitchen with mother where she had tea with her. Vicky pretended to read Newspaper. When she left, he shaved and took a bath. His prayers were heard and his faith in Vishnu remained unshakable. Moreover, she would come again, so he should always remain presentable at home.

His mother could notice the sudden change in the mood of his son. It was not wrong if a young man wants to look good and impress a beautiful young girl. But it would be blunder to expect anything more than this. It is better if she could warn him in time before it was too late. So he said to her son that Brahmin girls are to be revered by all people of other caste, and that it is a great sin to touch a Brahmin girl with malafide intentions. Vicky decided to proceed with caution.

She came the next day and then the day after that. He would wait for her to come. He would feel restless, if she did not come. They had become friendlier and she would discuss the book that he gave her to read. She developed new perspectives in the field of literature.

They knew their limitations. They were from different castes. They could never marry. However, who could stop them from dreaming? The dream is the only asset of a youth. They could dream without any censorship. No law or rule applies to see a dream, enjoy the freedom and see where it could take you.

Both of them talked misty-eyed, as if the world would end if they did not meet. The fire of passions had been lit, now it was only a matter of time when they would be burnt.

That was a cloudy day. The monsoon was expected any day. The life of the town depended on agriculture and the agriculture depended on monsoon. So clouds brought a wave of happiness on the faces of farmers, and the entire town was caught in the wave of jubilation and celebration of monsoon.

Megha had spent most of her childhood in the city and she did not know many people in the town. She had not even seen the temple of Hanumana. That day Vicky had offered her to show temple of Hanumana. When they were half the way, it started drizzling. Vicky suggested they take the shelter in the cave. Megha had not seen cave. They took the diversion that went up to the cave. They were wet but not entirely soaked. The rain became torrential. Due to the high velocity of wind, the showers of rain fell in waves and it even reached up to the terrace of the cave. Therefore, they entered the cave, which was comparatively warm. They felt safe and secluded.

Now they were cuddled in the cave. The noise of the storm and rainfall was deafening. Megha came closer to seek protection and Vicky embraced her in arms. She was trembling and her pink lips were inviting hesitant Vicky. She nibbled on his ears as if to give the green signal. Vicky bit her lower lip and she screamed. There was no pain, only pleasure.

It was strange, both of them knew they are not rebel type and they would marry the spouse their parents would decide for them, still they indulged into an act that was very immoral in the eyes of the society. When the storm of passion was over, the torrential rain diminished and the sky was clear when they were ready to climb down.

Both were well educated and they had taken a calculated risk. Megha was in her "safe period" and Vicky did not ejaculate inside. Both were voracious readers, so their togetherness would not create doubt. They had explored a new dimension of their relationship, so now when they talked about books as if it was based on their personal experience. They discussed Anna of "Anna caranina" of Leo Tolstoy, Scarlett O' Hara of "Gone with the wind" and Dominique of "Fountainhead" by Ayn Rand at length. They knew exactly what the author wants to say in the pretext of many similes and metaphors.

Megha had come for a week, but she told her parents that she would stay in the town till her college reopens. When all farmers were busy in tilling and sowing the land, the young couple tilled the body and mind and sowed it with crazy dreams. A crop they would never harvest.

One day when they were engaged in love making in the cave, a shepherd boy came to graze his cattle. He walked inside but the couple was so busy that they did not hear him coming closer. At that time luckily they were dressed and engaged in foreplay. The boy was about twelve years of age and was shocked to find someone unexpectedly. He shrieked and the couple unlocked from kiss and embrace.

Both were terrified. Vicky did not know the boy. He might have come from some other town to graze his cattle. He wanted to run away but Vicky caught hold of him. Vicky offered him some money but he refused to accept. Then Vicky threatened him if he says to anybody he would beat him. The boy got himself freed by jerks and ran down on the other side of the hill. Now Vicky was sure that the boy was not from his town because he climbed down on the other side of the hill. Everyone knew him in his own town.

They were afraid that how insulting it would be for both the families if it became a public issue. They were just wondering what they should do when the shepherd boy came with a constable and pointed at them. The constable came up to them and asked to follow him. All the four climbed down on the other side of the hill. On the midway where the cattle were grazing, the constable asked the boy to take care of cattle. The boy replied that the herd is in the habit to graze without a guard. It was obvious that the boy was interested in the fate of the couple. The couple was taken to the Police Station. The Station House Officer looked hard at them. He asked what they were doing in the cave. Vicky was literate and was aware that they were major and kissing was no crime. So he tried to be bold and said that this girl is her fiancée and they were going to Hanuman temple.

SHO asked the shepherd boy to go away, and asked the couple to sit. Vicky said that both of them study in college and any police inquiry would bring a disgrace to the family. Police Officer wanted to fill up a form and wanted two guarantors. Megha who had remained silent so far, intervened and asked Police Officer why does he want to defame her.

The Police Officer also had a daughter of marriageable age. Vicky had already given references of two police officials. They appeared scared and innocent. The Police Officer was experienced and could judge the criminals by face. He decided that the couple belonged to a reputed family and it would not be wise to tarnish their image.

Vicky saw hesitation on the face of Police Officer and took out his wallet from the pocket. He had only fifty-rupee note in it. He gave it to Police Officer. The Police Officer shook his head but did not return the money. Vicky knew if he accepts the money, they could go. Police Officer took his mobile number in case the father of the girl files any complaint. When they were out of Police Station, they did not climb the hill but returned home by bus.

Next day Megha returned to the city without bidding farewell to Vicky. It was not strange; Vicky had a gut feeling that, that was their last meeting. Their love story was fated to a tragic end, but it would be so soon and blunt, they did not expect.

He remembered when they were in the cave he had told Megha "I love you" and Megha was astonished to hear these words. She raised her brows and said "really"? He had pondered for a few minutes before he replied, "Yes, and exact opposite of whatever I say is also equally true", and she had laughed.

After the episode, Vicky decided to go and work in the city and study privately. Megha had kindled his desire to knowledge and wisdom both.

The city life was the dream of every youth in the town. The only criterion of success for them was money. Those who were intelligent in studies saw the dream to become doctors, engineers, management executives and civil servants. Those who found books repulsive would dream to become a businessperson. The mediocre and those who could not afford higher studies would work in departmental stores, malls, factories and shops. Some of them had entrepreneur skills, learned the tricks of the trade, the availability of cheaper goods, display, inventory control, promoting business, importance of customer satisfaction, and later or sooner would open their own shop.

Bhola was a dimwit but his wife Usha was a quick learner and ambitious. She had no patience to become rich. She had a gut feeling for good proposals. However, she was uneducated, but she was intelligent. She knew beauty and youth were her assets. She thought Bhola was an ideal husband for her. He never interfered in her thirst for extravagant adventures. She knew what kind of friends she would need to be successful, and why they would become her friend. She selected those middle-aged mature people who lacked excitement in their life. Soon she was a friend of a bank manager, a civil servant, a property dealer, a goldsmith and a school owner.

Later on when she became millionaire, she abandoned them and made a new friend circle with a politician, an Industrialist, a hotel owner and a real estate agent. She did not waste time in developing friendship with doctors and advocates because she knew the best could be hired at any odd hour. These professionals expected fees even from friends. The success is a vague term, and everyone has a different perception of it. The gross stupid generalization would be that money is the only criterion of success.

Usha was a source of inspiration for many town girls. Their parents would give them her example. Only if they knew how she climbed the stairs of success. Then, everyone has to make some compromises if one is too ambitious to reach to the top quickly. Only hard work, labor, sincerity and commitment would never take you there unless you have the tact to exploit, manipulate and circumvent to achieve the target. Teenage is the best age for a girl; a boy has his best years in early youth when he runs in the twenties. Boys are more awkward with their thin line hairs above the upper lip and a tuft of hairs on the chin. Girls even in early teens take pride and feel boosted by tiny breast and information that they have gathered about periods.
They feel a new emotional attachment with grown up women, elder sisters, sister-in –laws and aunts.

Town girls are no exception. When Usha came to visit her parents in town, many young girls visited her house and even invited her to their home despite the fact that she was of a lower caste. Their parents did not appreciate it but they kept silent since Usha had good connection with district administration, especially with the officers who belonged to lower caste and reached to higher position due to reservation in government jobs. Such officers were very helpful to people of their own community. They would go out of the way to support and promote people of their own caste even at the cost of the people of the upper caste. In their subconscious mind, they have a revengeful attitude against the people of upper caste, especially the Brahmins. Traditionally Warriors were neutral about them and Tradesmen gave them money on loan, during hardship, so it was only Brahmins who were their sworn enemies. They had declared them untouchable and did not permit them to enter temples. They would give references of Sanskrit scriptures, which illiterate villagers would easily believe.

Usha helped in resolving problems of the villagers about Below Poverty Line card, which was a big asset of poor and downtrodden families. If once, the card was issued, after some administrative jugglery, the owner was entitled to many pecuniary benefits of free food grains and interest free loans. Even those who were not so poor to be entitled to the BPL card, made efforts to obtain one. Many genuine people suffered since they did not have influence on Patwari who is Land record keeper or they did not belong to the group of the Headman of the village. Usha knew the hierarchy of the administration and did little string pulling of the right authority to set the things in motion. She motivated young girls for education and helped their parents in searching a suitable match for their girls in the city. Villagers consulted her before litigation and usually she would resolve the issue out of court. It saved time and money for both the parties.

Only a few years back, Bhadrajun, the native place of Usha, was a small village. Due to proximity to the city and a politically powerful Headman of the village, many amenities like senior secondary school, post office, bank, hospital and a community center were developed. So many times, it is difficult to differentiate a town from the village. The difference is not only of facilities, but also of mentality. A town is big enough to be called a village but is smaller than a city. People of town are no more simpleton as in the village nor are they as smart as in the city. Villagers live contended life; but in towns, people have ambitions, which are the enemy of contentment. Youth from town and villages flock together in cities, with one motto– to stand taller than their city counterparts.

Rural young men and their mannerism awe the city girls. Boys of some farmer's caste are crazy after girls. They would try to entice the girls by traditional methods of praising them. Initially the girls would object but slowly their ears are poisoned by words of flattery and their objections become soft and inviting. Then the boys would offer flowers and chocolates, which were created by God with the sole purpose of helping young men to entice girls. You would never see a girl refusing to either of them, especially if the presenter had been praising them day and night (in dreams) for a long time. Some village girls also reach up to college level in the cities but they never take interest in city boys. Most of them are of studious type and wear such clumsy cloth, which daunt their beauty to the extent of ugliness.

The Rajput or warrior boys never run after city girls. They would spend their time in the gymnasium and they would maintain the internal protocol of their clan. The King of the state awarded the titles to the members of the clan long back during the feudal system, depending upon the ownership of the size of the land and proximity to the king. The clan still maintained the legacy of those titles, though after independence, democratic Indian government took the title of king away and hence title awarded by the Kings had become meaningless. The folks in the villages and towns still revered those titles, despite the fact that many landowners had sold their land due to bad habits of liquor and gambling and had almost become pauper.

Some girls especially of Brahmin community did not like skinny Brahmin boys. These boys were brought up in cultured families where women were worshipped and the food was vegetarian to curb the sexual desires. Brahmin girls were attracted towards macho Rajput boys who had muscular bodies and flamboyant style.

Sanjana Mishra was a cute looking Brahmin girl who was class fellow of Usha in Primary School. The father of Sanjana was an employee of Food Corporation of India, posted at Bhadrajun at that time. He was a simple God-fearing man who was a staunch devotee of celibate God Hanuman. He had made a folk orchestra to sing prayers on Tuesday. The group was so popular that it was booked for all Tuesdays throughout the year. He was in demand even in nearby areas. Sanjana's father was transferred in the nearby city after few years he had worked in the town. Usha was married to Bhola and came to live in the city, and then she inquired about Sanjana.

She was surprised that Sanjana was altogether a different girl. She looked like modern city girls. Her dress up revealed her neckline of heavy bosom and she wore skirt exposing her marble white cylindrical thighs. While talking, she used many English words. She was pleased to meet her childhood friend. A childhood friend is an asset and should never be ignored. Usha had seen Sanjana many times with a handsome young man on a motorbike. Usha talked with Bhola about her friend. Bhola told her that Sanjana was in the wrong company. The young handsome man was a Rajput popularly called Tutu Banna. He was called so because his right wrist was damaged when his enemies attacked him at midnight with a sword and tried to cut off his hands. He lived in Rajput Hostel. He changed his girlfriends with the change of season. Which meant he would have at least half a dozen girlfriends in a year leaving one nightstand aside. Still girls flocked around him and were proud to be seen with him in his open jeep that screeched on the roads of the new campus of the university where Faculty of Arts was located, or would sit on the backseat of his motorbike almost glued to his back with one hand on his shoulder and other idly placed on his crotch. When he would apply the brakes of motorbike suddenly their bosom would crush on his back and by the time they would get down from motorbike their erected tits would be visible through their toppers. It was combined effect of the speed of the motorbike, masculine aroma of Banna and frequent crushing of their bosoms on the back of Banna.

Sanjana Mishra like all the past conquests of Banna was an exceptionally beautiful girl. She belonged to a middle class family, her father was an inspector in Food Corporation of India. The gifts of costly mobiles, purse and fashionable dresses impressed her. Once when she was late to reach the rendezvous due to crowded city bus, her boyfriend got so impatient that when she reached there, he first took her to a motorbike show room and gifted her scooter of her choicest brand. That day she gifted him her virginity. Tutu Banna must have smiled in his heart; no girl could resist his charms infinitely. Once he throws the grains before a bird, it is only a matter of time when would she picks it. When Banna would reach a saturation level with the girl, he would place her before his friends. He believed in sharing. He never bothered for easily achievable girls. The harder the girls made it , the greater was the fun for Banna.

The ex-girlfriends of Banna were safe from any eve teasing, pass or vulgar comments from ragamuffins of the college. Ordinary boys who came to college for studies would avoid them. The girls of rich and cultured families who secretly called such girls as "current account" also avoided them. The boys were like eagle, which flew high in the sky but could detect a rat moving on earth. The human being has an animal instinct so far as detection of a pray is concerned. After that, it is just a matter of time.

Usha and Sanjana were birds of the same feather. They had similar moral values and opinion about society. Both flew high in their own sphere without a trespass of their boundaries since the object of one was fun while that of another was money or social contacts, which can be encashed in future. They sought guidance from each other and learned the secrets of manipulating chauvinistic males to fulfill their own ulterior motives.

Is destiny more powerful than manipulation ? On one such destined day Usha in the Mall introduced Vicky to Sanjana. Sanjana had to buy cosmetics and Usha came to collect her due payment. When Usha introduced Sanjana and Vicky, Sanjana offered her hand to shake. This is quite uncommon in most of the urban areas of India. In metropolitan cities, youth is accustomed to western style and mannerism but for Vicky it was an awkward moment and he unwillingly extended his hand. She shook his hand warmly and held it in a tight grip, an act certainly not expected from a girl on her first introduction. Vicky's mind was drawing some fast conclusions and in a way, he felt that this girl was either a challenge or a threat to his masculinity. Vicky was perplexed for a moment but then he decided it was a challenge and he should accept it. He looked into the eyes of the girl and while she was still shaking his hand. He squeezed her hand with a force and she had a smile of victory on her face. When she loosened her grip, Vicky twisted his index finger and rubbed it in the center of her palm. The message was well received and immediately her cheeks became pink, eyes lowered and lips quivered from shyness.

Now it was Vicky's turn to smile.

Usha was oblivious of what was going on between her two best friends. She was busy in tracing the manager who would pass her bill for payment, and when finally she saw him on a counter she left in his direction hurriedly without bothering to bid farewell.

The hours of early morning are dull in any mall. Vicky was free since there was no customer on counter. He called a bellhop to deliver three cups of tea and offered a stool to Sanjana to sit down. Sanjana kept on standing. She forgot that she had come to buy cosmetics. Usha returned disappointed, the Manager had asked her to come after a week for payment. All the three sipped tea silently. Usha asked her friend to buy cosmetics, but Sanjana refused. She had an awkward inventory of cosmetics to buy; she would die of shame asking for it from Vicky. She could still feel his scratching index finger in the soft muscles of shallow of her palm. How indicative, innovative and suggestive his gesture was.

Usha started telling Sanjana that she was in urgent need of money to pay to workers. In a way she wanted to remind Vicky that he should return her overdue loan. Vicky pretended to remain busy in arranging his counter; he had no money to return to Usha. His heartbeat had become fast and he felt some perspiration on his face. Usha offered him herhandkerchief to dry his face. Vicky did not accept it, but he could not dare to pull out his own handkerchief from his pocket, since it was dirty. Usha knew Vicky is feeling embarrassed because of her friend, Sanjana. Even while searching for Manager, she had noticed an instant chemistry between them. It was a good occasion to humiliate Vicky. Sanjana presumed that her friend is trying to borrow some money from her. She opened her purse and took out a few hundred rupees that she had and offered to her friend. Usha refused to accept money. Her object of insulting Vicky had already been served.

All the three had minor disappointment since morning. The manager had refused to make payment to Usha, Sanjana could not buy her cosmetics some of which she urgently required, and Usha once again humiliated Vicky for money. Thankfully, Usha did not insult him before her friend. Vicky came outside the Mall to see them off. The weather was fine, clouds were drifting in the light blue sky and slow wind was blowing. After the heat of the last few days, it was pleasant to feel the cold wind on the skin.

They had no business to remain together, Usha had to go back to her home, Sanjana had to attend a class in College, and Vicky should have returned to his counter. All the three stood as if glued to each other. None of them wanted to depart. Usha had no work at home, her son would come in the afternoon from the school and her brother would take care of him, Sanjana had no interest in the lecture and even if she reached to college, she was sure she would not attend the lecture. Vicky had no customers, moreover now he had an assistant and was comparatively relaxed.

Usha came forward to rescue them. She suggested that they should go to Vicky's room, fry some onion rings and potato chips, and celebrate the weather. Sanjana and Vicky felt relieved and happy. Usha was glad that her scheme was successful. She had seen some porn movies and orgy was her fantasy. God willing, she would be able to fulfill her dream with her best friends. Vicky said he would take permission from the Manager. All the three started walking towards Vicky's room. On their way, Vicky bought onion, potato and a cane of edible oil. He walked a little faster to reach home before Usha and Sanjana, to put it in order. The girls were happy that Vicky was behaving like awed teenager.

Usha took the command and checked the stove. It has only a little kerosene left. Vicky did not have it in stock, so Usha asked him to bring from the market. Vicky lifted two-liter jarricane and left for market. Both the girls giggled when he scuttled out of the door.

Once on the street, Vicky felt his heart beat faster in the presence of Sanjana. Actually, Sanjana was more beautiful than his dream girl. The length and taper of her chiseled nose was in fine proportion to her big inviting eyes, rosy cheeks and a pert pair of lips. The other most significant part of her beauty were her earlobes. The cartilage was pink and translucent, and the lower end was delicately holding a thin earring. She is the girl he could die for.

Now he felt nervous, what she would feel about him by looking at his room. It reflected a poor style of living. The most precious things in his room were books. She did not look like book reader. She would definitely discard him. She has come not because of him, but at the request of her fast friend. At the most, she may have some curiosity how does a bachelor boy live. On his way, he crossed the liquor shop. He had money enough only to buy kerosene or a quarter of whisky. The kerosene shop would give him on credit but the liquor shop did not sell on credit. He went to a liquor shop and bought a quarter of whisky. The shop owner knew him well, so he gave him a glass and a bottle of water from the refrigerator. He did not touch the glass, opened the bottle and drank half of it neat. The whisky made a line of fire from his throat to stomach which was one of the most pleasant sensation for him. He filled the bottle with iced water and finished in two gulps. He felt that his nervousness was gone and his palms were no more perspiring.

Usha and Sanjana had cut onion rings and potato chips to deep fry after dipping in gram flour paste. When he entered the room and set down beside them to fill up a stove tank, both the girls looked in each other's eyes. They could know by smell that he had taken drinks. They did not mind it. Sanjana had taken drinks with her Rajput friends and Usha was acquainted with it since childhood.

By the time the first lot of onion and potatoes was fried, it started raining. Vicky had a collection of old romantic songs on his mobile and he started playing it. There was no fresh plate to serve and Vicky wanted to wash some soiled plates, but Usha picked up an old newspaper and poured the stuff on it. She said newspaper would soak extra oil and they would be able to watch calories. Sanjana was thinner than Usha. The beauty of Usha was in her suppleness and that of Sanjana in her perfect body; in any case, both were equally sensual.

By the time they finished their snacks and tea, the rain had stopped and all the three of them had business to attend to, so they departed bidding goodbye.

Infosys selected Kiran in campus placement. She came to meet Vicky before she left for Bangalore. She took a promise from him that he would finish his post graduation and would prepare for civil service examination. Vicky nodded his head but Kiran insisted him to repeat the words of promise. Vicky resolved in his heart to buy the books earliest possible, since dates of examination were coming closer. First, he would try to get them free or on loan from some acquaintance, then he would try second hand book depot. Buying a fresh textbook stood last on his choice.

He disliked one-week series, which was so popular amongst students. It has chapters based on last five-year question papers. Out of ten units, every student prepared five units since out of ten questions, one from each unit, only five were to be attempted. Vicky did his studies in different style. He would read all units, would never ask for important questions from his day scholar friends, would read reference books, and published research papers in journals on the topics of his interest. He decided to take his weekly off from Mall on Monday and spend the day in the library of the university, to consult reference books and journals.

He remembered Megha had told him about her friends who were pursuing post graduation in English Literature. The memories of the time spent with Megha made him melancholic. He would recede in his somber mood, followed by depression. In such a mood, he would resort to alcohol and the vicious cycle would make him schizoid for at least a fortnight.

With this expectation, Vicky was arranging cosmetics on his counter. The Manager had seen that girls and women were always attracted towards him. His melancholic look worked as a magnet and he looked more seductive to affluent girls who thought they could buy happiness with money. Just to impress him they would buy costly cosmetics, even if it is not required. For Vicky they did not matter. He did not like the odor of deodorant, perfumes, talcum powder and scents.

Sometimes they would seek his suggestion to draw his attention but he would point out the costliest one without applying his mind, for he knew that such girls always presumed that costly brands are always of better quality. One must learn to pay for better things in one's life.

In the middle row, he kept creams like "Boro Plus, Fair and Lovely" which were very popular in middle and lower middle class families. They were fast moving products as Indian young girls were obsessed with white skin. The friends were competitor to look whiter and they applied all types of fairness creams and domestic formulae, which claimed to be a remedy for the ailment of dark skin. Vicky never thought white as beautiful. He would rather prefer a girl with brown lustrous skin and had good features and figures. Usually beautiful girls devoted much energy of their mind in memorizing compliments they received that their IQ level went down. It would be a waste of the day if nobody complimented them and would never wear a dress again, whatever may be the cost, if even a single friend criticized it, on the day they wear it first.

He was looking down at the arrangement of cosmetics with a satisfaction when he heard a melodious voice asking him

"Do you have bathing soap Dove"?

He first saw the reflection in the glass of the counter; he could not believe his eyes, that it was Megha.

He looked up slowly, as he did not trust his luck. He wanted to prolong the moment when he believed he was near his heartthrob Megha. Both were unable to control their emotions when their eyes met. Many colors came and went on their faces. When Megha spoke after long moments, her voice was husky and eyes were moist.

"How are you"?
"I am fine" Vicky replied in weak and trembling voice.

He had never been so nervous before. They had never met after an awkward incident, when Police caught them after lovemaking in a cave. Vicky felt more ashamed today than he had felt that day. Sometimes a gap intensifies the emotions. If you scratch the cover of a healing wound, it becomes more painful.

"What do you want"? Vicky wanted to treat her as customer to save embarrassment.

She looked into his hollow eyes and felt weak in her knees. She sat down on a stool holding her head in hands. Slowly she bowed her head on the counter and fainted. Vicky rushed and brought a glass of water. He sprinkled some water on her face. Some salespersons and customers assembled around the girl. Each had his own opinion about the situation and remedy. Vicky lifted her in his arms and took her to the Manager's cabin. When he put her down on the sofa, she regained her consciousness.

Due to rain one day before, humidity and suffocation were at peak. Vicky asked a bellhop to bring cold drinks in glasses. Megha sipped and felt better. Vicky did not touch his drink. He offered Megha to escort her to home which she refused. She opened her purse and took out her mobile. She asked for Vicky's number and dialed. Vicky received a miss call and saved her number. He walked with her up to the lounge where Megha stopped and asked him to go back.

He came back to his counter. His melancholy had sublimated in anxiety. Megha could not bear the stress and hence fainted. Vicky thought he was responsible for such condition of the girl. The pang of guilt pierced his heart. The only consolation was that he was not alone in trauma Megha was with him. If they would share their agony, one day they would be happy together. Despite the shock, Megha had managed to exchange mobile number, as if a drowning man catches at a straw. What a relief. Vicky took out his mobile and looked at the missed call number, as if it was his lifeline.

Next day at 8.00 A.M. when Vicky was getting ready to go to the Mall on his duty, the number blinked with a ring on his mobile. He had saved it as Meh to hide her identity and ultimately this piece of cloud (megha) was like a shower (meh) in the deserts of his life. Megha apologized for having fainted day before, he apologized for shocking her to that extent. He invited her to the University library where he was visiting the next day to borrow a few books on the card of his friend. She agreed to meet him at stipulated time under a Neem tree outside the library.

Both reached the same place from different directions simultaneously. She was looking astoundingly beautiful in her crimson and yellow combination of Salwar Kameez that gave her a glow of setting sun. Only a literature student can have that aesthetic sense. Vicky wore a blue denim jeans, lemon yellow T-shirt and sports shoes. He carried a shoulder bag filled with books, a notebook and loose papers.

The trauma of a day before was over, and they were in a happy mood. Dense trees surrounded the library and weather was perfect for longing couple. The campus was deserted except one or two couples seen gossiping under a tree. The hawk-cuckoo also known as Papiha broke the silence of the campus in their sweet voice. Usually birds make that special sound to attract their mating counterparts. The call is pee-kaha or "where is my love" acts as catalyst for a forlorn heart of love seekers.

They gossiped about everything, Vicky told her about his job, his future plan for post graduation, about Usha, Kiran and Sanjana. Megha knew about these girls from the village and had no doubt that none of them was good enough for Vicky. Usha was promiscuous; Kiran and Sanjana were seen in the company of vagabond Rajput boys. Vicky in her opinion was a man of refined taste. Since he was a thorough gentle man, he may not refuse the company of these girls when they approached to him, since they belonged to the same village, but he would never relish being in their company. The faith is a necessary element of strong bonding.

Before departing Vicky asked her for books of M.A., (Previous) English Literature and she promised she would collect them from her friend for him.
Next day at about 7.00 PM, he received a SMS.

"I have collected two books, how can I deliver them to you"?

"Meet me outside the Mall at 8 P.M." he replied.

"My parents won't permit after sunset" she had a point.

"Can I come somewhere near your home," he was desperate.

"Oh no, please never come near my home," she was scared.

"Don't worry, I won't. But tell me how can I collect the books, I need them badly," he made an excuse to meet.

"If you can come at Coasters, the coffee shop near your mall, you can meet me. I have your books with me" Megha made an offer.

"OK, I reach there within five minutes" his heart pounded she was just in the adjacent building.

When Vicky reached in Coasters, Megha was taking Coffee with her friend. She introduced her to Vicky. Her name was Shalini and her nickname was Shalu. She was in the final year of M.A. English Literature. She could lend him her books of the previous year for one year, after that she would take an examination of National Educational Testing for lecturership and she would need her books back then. Vicky gladly accepted the help as he was sure he would clear the examination in first attempt. She had already brought two books, which Megha handed him over. Vicky knew if he stayed longer and accepted the offer of coffee he would have to pay for it, and he did not have enough money in his pocket, so he begged an excuse pretending rush on his counter. The girls accepted his excuse as genuine and bid him bye with a promise to meet again soon.

It was sooner than he had expected. Next day at about 9.00 A.M., Megha walked into the mall straight to his counter when Vicky was still dusting and arranging the cosmetics. He had made it clear to her that she should not come to the mall, if Bhola or Usha would see her, they may talk to her parents. Though Vicky believed they would never do anything like this but it was an excuse to save his own face as he worked on cosmetics counter and did a couple of odd jobs, one of which he was doing right now.

She carried many books in her lap and put them on his counter, and said, "These books cover the whole syllabus and now you must do some hard work like a good boy". Vicky could not restrain his smile on her style of command. Her sincerity and innocence was heart touching. He collected all books and placed them in a drawer under counter. He promised he would start his studies from today. She smiled back and left in hurry for college.

Vikram was sitting idle on the counter when he decided to look at the books at a glance.

There were ten books besides two given yesterday. He picked up "Paradise Lost" by John Milton, and turned pages.

She had underlined few sentences, "solitude sometimes is best society". He thought about himself. He always preferred solitude. After few more pages she had underlined

"Grace was in all her steps, Heaven in her eye, In every gesture, dignity and love."

That was Megha! Why her friend would underline it? She must be thinking about herself. Vicky saw the first page of the book. In ornamental handwriting, her name Shalini Agarwal was written in blue-black ink. He had once read a book on handwriting analysis. The right slant of the words means she liked to socialize and small words meant she could focus. The pointed S indicated that she was intellectually probing; her L and E had loops indicating she was open mind. Moreover, the surname Agarwal suggested that she was of his caste. Vicky did not remember anything special about her since he had spent only five minutes with her in Coasters. She was beautiful and spoke only few words. Next time he would like to know more about his benefactor.

Vicky turned pages of all the books rapidly. The books were well maintained, had her name on the first page and only few lines were underlined. Vicky never liked to underline anything in his books. For the first time he liked the books that were underlined. It looked as if she is communicating with him through these underlines. What type of woman would have dignity and love in her every gesture. Usha had no dignity when she made sexual gestures. She preferred to go wild. Vicky loved dignity in every gesture and the rare combination of dignity and love. The more he contemplated on it, the more remorse took over him.

The monsoon had hit the city. Since morning, it was drizzling, and sales were slumped, so he decided to retreat in his room with a quarter of whisky. He informed his manager that he would return in afternoon and left. He bought one-quarter bottle of whisky on his way to his room. The drizzling turned into heavy rain by the time he reached his room.

When he was about to finish his first bottle, the mobile blinked. It was Meh. She presumed that he was in the Mall but was surprised when he told her that he was at his room. He made an excuse that he was not well, so he has come to his room to rest. Megha insisted to come to her room. He was in no mood to receive Megha in his small one room house, but she threatened to ask Usha, so he gave his address. After few minutes, she was in his apartment.

Vicky made no efforts to make the room look decent. His mood was too somber for that. Megha sat down beside him on the floor where he was lying on his back on a thin mattress. She put her hand on his forehead to check if he had fever. His temperature was normal. She checked her throat and wrist for temperature. He had no fever. She looked in his eyes and blinked. He remembered "Heaven in her eyes", how true it was for her. He held her hand put it over his heart. His heart was throbbing with full velocity. She could feel it with her palm. At that moment Vicky thought of death. If he dies at this moment, he would have no regrets. The expression on the face of Megha had already given a meaning to his otherwise futile life. He puts his own hand over hand of Megha, and they remained like that for moments that could be stretched to eternity.

Slowly when her hands are on his chest, exactly on heart, she lies down beside him without removing her hand. Two slander beautiful bodies were lying side by side on a mattress.

As if to communicate heart to heart, he placed his hand on her left breast.

The heartthrob was violent and he could feel it despite the massive mound of her breast.

The effect of alcohol took over him, and slowly and gently he started squeezing the breast he was holding. Hand of Megha was no more glued to left side of chest but was roaming with luster and grace on the topography of his body.

Heart, body, mind and soul search for compatibility. Even if one of them is successful, the life reaches to a blissful fulfillment. Vicky thought Megha was compatible at all levels of his existence and there is nothing beyond their union in this cosmos. The music created by rain was a witness to their ecstasy, and music was still playing so they remained in that united position until it stopped. Megha dressed while sitting on mattress, but Vicky had no strength to get up and bid her farewell so he just waved his hand, stretched his body on the space vacated by Megha on the mattress and snorted. Megha covered his naked body by a bedcover and left.

The Central library of the university became their regular meeting place. First, they would hangout near library to update each other about friends, families and studies, and then they would occupy seats in library for serious studies. They would sit neither too far nor too near, so that occasionally they could look at each other and pass a smile. Megha read the books of Sanskrit Literature, and Vicky prepared notes from the books of English Literature. Sometimes when they read something that touched their heart they looked up simultaneously, and smiled to acknowledge the telepathy.

When they came out of the library, it was drizzling. They left their books and notebooks on the reception of library and walked together. They were discussing how Sanskrit was the only grammatically perfect language. Megha explained the six tenses and said there is no present continuous tense in the Sanskrit grammar. Vicky was of the opinion that there is no present tense as such, what has happened is past and what is going to happen is future. He gave example of their walking. When he lifts a leg it is past, when he puts it forward is future, so there is no present.

The weather was cloudy, Megha asked if Vicky had read "Meghdootam", Vicky had read all three plays written by Kalidas, said he liked them very much. He asked Megha to recite her favourite verses. Megha recited a verse from Kumarsambhva in which drop of first monsoon rain falls on meditating Uma .

"With momentary pause the first drop rest
Upon her lash then strike her nether lip,
Fracture upon the highland of her breast,
Across the ladder of her waist than trip
And slowly at her naval comes to rest. "
(Translation by Ingalls)

Her voice was melodious and her pronunciations were accurate. To Vicky she looked like an embodiment of Uma herself. The raindrops that fell on her face traveled from her long eyelashes to pouting lower lip, to hard breast large enough to touch each other and were lost in the deep neckline. Megha could feel his eyes are tracing raindrop and her cheeks became pink with shy. This enhanced her beauty several times and she stopped when rain drop finally rested in the deep naval of Uma in the poem. Alas! Vicky had no way to trace the raindrop on Megha's body since she wore a Salwar-Kameeze , but the thought occurred simultaneously in their mind and Megha's pinkness of cheeks descended up to the toes of her feet.

Vicky was talking about the spiritual meaning of the verse to hide his nervousness. He believed the poet wants to use the physical beauty of the Goddess as symbolic to the contours of the mother Goddess Earth and its fertility. Megha was too unnerved to react to what Vicky was saying, but his explanation gave her enough time to regain her composure.

They silently moved back to the library and collected their bags from reception to depart.

Vicky and Megha were students of the subject they loved. Reading was not burden for them but an enjoyable activity. They were happy in comparison to those who read the subjects they had no interest in but were good for career. High remunerative jobs were easily available to students of engineering and management. Many students were cramming formulas of Physics and Mathematics day and night to succeed in the entrance examination and get a branch which had a better career option. Then their whole life would be nothing but a rat race.

Vicky and Megha did not have craze to live an affluent life. They believed in that happiness which money cannot buy. Nevertheless, they were ambitious and prepared to exploit their potential to realize their self-esteem. Both of them saw a dream to work together in the department of languages under faculty of arts in the university. Only if their parents allowed they could make an ideal couple. However, their parents were traditional and they would never allow inter-caste marriage, and thus if they see any dream like that it is bound to be shattered by the hard realities of life.

Who can stop a person to see a dream, howsoever impossible it may be. Therefore, despite the fact that all the odds were against them, they saw dreams in their own eyes and in the eyes of each other. They would spend hours chatting on mobile and sending pictures, messages, status updates and emails. They shared activities of various literature groups on social websites and blogs. Thus, they were in a live - together relationship in their cyber life.

In "Paradise Lost" John Milton has described how Eve was tempted by Satan to eat the forbidden apple and eve induced Adam to pluck the apple and eat it with her. Both became aware of their nakedness and world ensued. Despite having heard this story innumerable time, Eves are still tempted and Adams are still induced to act against their conscience and join the act in desperation.

When Megha offered they went to the theater to watch a movie. Vicky knew it would be wrong to fall to this temptation. He did not protest. Whatever argument he might give to avoid being together in public places, Megha must have already considered it and when as a girl she was ready to take risks, why he should hesitate. Therefore, he consented and instead of going to the library, they went to watch a latest super hit Bollywood movie in the theater.

Initially Usha thought Vicky is avoiding her since he was serious in his preparation for examination. Later on, she realized that Vicky is hiding and something fishy is going on. She decided to find out. She made it a point to stay at his counter for a talk whenever she came to the mall. One day luck favoured her. Vicky had gone for washroom and Usha was waiting at his counter when she saw that Vicky had left his mobile in the open drawer of the counter and it was blinking. She bent on the counter. The screen displayed that call was from Meh. She didn't know any Meh, but she was sure that the call was from some girl and she is the reason why Vicky is avoiding her.

Jealousy is like a cat, she walks silently and belligerently. Usha had learned many things from her pet cat, and one of them was to wait for the right moment patiently. When Vicky came back from the washroom, he saw Usha on his counter. He picked up his mobile and checked, there was a missed call. He thanked his good luck that he had saved the number of Megha by pseudo name. He had observed that day-by-day Usha had become more inquisitive about his activities and her questions dug deep in his personal life. When she did not ask him about Meh, he became suspicious. Both looked into the eyes of each other, Usha accusingly and Vicky defensively.

Everything fell into place when Usha saw Vicky and Megha in the cinema hall. Usha herself was with a distant cousin who was her secret lover, so she did not go near them. She was sitting in the last row of the balcony and just behind her Megha and Vicky were sitting in a box. The box had more privacy and they were sitting on the sofa which provided them the opportunity to take liberties. Her cousin was a handsome young guy, who had recently come from a village. He was very shy in taking initiative and Usha knew she would have to maneuver him first; once he is aroused there would be no stopping him. Now she was distracted and her game plan was spoiled. The cat had taken her possession. She could see the depth of their relationship. The way Megha doted on Vicky and he glued to her intimately, it was obvious that they have crossed the limits of being friends.

The cousin of Usha thought that he has said something to displease her and she is no more eager to take any advantage of the situation. They had managed to take a corner seat in the last row, which is safe for all types of sensual activities. He wanted to put her back in the mood, but he was a novice and did not know how to do it. He put his arm around her and his fingers touched her breast but she did not react. Slowly he increased his efforts, but nothing registered in the mind of Usha. The wall between balcony and box was high and even if she stood up, she would not be able to see what was going on inside box. She had seen no other couple-entering the box, so she presumed that they were the only couple in the box, which had four sofas for four couples.

Once she had also seen a movie with Vicky in the same box, without anyone around and they had taken full advantage of privacy. Now that Vicky was sitting with a Brahmin girl who in her opinion had no skill required in a woman to please her man. The cousin lost his patience and squeezed her hard; she could not restrain a shriek, got up and left the theater before the interval. Cousin followed her.

Usha hired an auto taxi from outside the theater for her home. Her cousin toddled behind her and jumped in an auto taxi lest she leave him behind. He was still perplexed and could find no reason that may offend Usha. He saw Usha as an idol who had succeeded in the urban concrete jungle where survival of the fittest was the first law. A lower caste illiterate woman was fighting her way and climbing the stairs of success and to reach at the top was her only ambition in life.

The name of the cousin was Gulaba Ram. He had finished his senior secondary school from town and had come to the city to study. His family background was poor and he was living in a free hostel provided by government to the boys of lower community who come to the city for higher studies. Usha had assured him that she would manage a scholarship from the Social Welfare department for him due to her contacts in district administration. Gulaba believed her and Usha used him to run the errands for her. Gulaba was young and handsome and to have him at her mercy was a big gratification for Usha.

When they reached home, Usha paid for the taxi and went inside her home. She fell down on her bed and hid her face in the pillow. Secretly she shed tear. Tears wash all the frustration of watching Vicky with Megha. Gulaba prepared tea in the kitchen and brought in a tray for her. She was touched by his sincerity and concern. His evening was unnecessarily spoiled. She knew he was anticipating fun and had tried to draw her attention. Being a novice, he did not know that when a woman is not in mood to yield, do not try hard. That is the space they need. Sometimes you are able to seduce a woman by trying not to seduce her.

Buddha said "Unfathomly deep, deep like a fish course in water is the character of woman."

Gulaba didn't know anything about all these things, he concluded that Usha was in a bad mood and he had seen his father pampering his mother when she was in a bad mood. Therefore, he had gone to the kitchen and prepared a cardamom tea, which was Usha's favorite. Usha felt pity for the boy and resolved to compensate him some other day. Meanwhile, unexpectedly Gulaba set down near the feet of Usha on the bed and started pressing her legs with his palm. Children usually do this to parents or grandparents to appease and seek blessings from them. In a way, it is the higher kind of submission. Usha protested unwillingly since she was enjoying his act. He kept on doing it until she dozed off. Then Gulaba left for his hostel.

Vicky did not impress Sanjana. That day she went to his room because her fast friend Usha requested her. The room was more disappointing than Vicky. She disliked poverty and lower standards of living. She did not bother to look at books as she knew books had no meaning in her life. She had realized that even a best couplet defining beauty is nowhere near to pleasure that it can give. All the praise of feminine beauty in poetry is a way of seducing them by males to fulfill their ulterior motive. She would prefer a paramour who bestows diamond jewelry on her rather than a poor poet who writes sonnets about her beauty.

When she met Usha that evening and found her in a bad mood, she could know that cat is hurt. It takes cat to know another. Usha confessed everything to her. Despite having the same approach towards life, she knew Usha had a weakness for Vicky. Had Vicky confided in her about his relationship with Megha, Usha might not have felt so hurt. Any act done secretly from the friends hurts their ego and they want to make you look down for that. You can choose your friends, but you cannot choose your enemies.

When Sanjana met Vicky that day with Usha she was mesmerized by his intense look and depth in his eyes. When she saw his room where he lived without any facilities like an animal, and returned drunk when he went to market, the talisman was broken and she could know that he was a loser. She despised loser and thought it was a contagious disease more heinous than leprosy. Therefore, if he has broken the confidence of her friend, she did not mind if he suffers the consequences.

If one cat can shake a man two cats can shake his whole world. Usha and Sanjana made a plan to make Vicky look down, for what in their eyes was his irresponsible behavior.

In the same evening Megha was sitting with her friend Shalini in their favorite café Coasters, Megha told her that she went to watch a movie with Vicky. Shalini asked how was the movie and Megha replied spontaneously that she does not know. Shalini could deduce but laughed at her frank admittance. For a long time they discussed the couplets of Sanskrit and English poetry that describes the turmoil of beloved damsel pierced by golden arrows of Cupid.

Love tends to schemes, positive schemes make life heaven, negative kills. Four girls were scheming at this moment, Usha and Sanjana to destroy the affair between Vicky and Megha, and Shalini and Megha to resolve the wound created by a golden tip arrow of cupid.

After long discussions and rejecting various plans on the ground of risk of exposure involved and quantum of damage caused, Usha finally concluded that they should write a letter to parents of Megha in the village rather than to maternal grandparents with whom Megha lived in the city. They were old and heart patient and such news could be dangerous for them while Megha's father was a priest in the temple and was known as strict and traditional. Usha had taken a picture of Megha and Vicky while they were waiting in the lounge of theater. They had bought an ice-cream cone from a vendor and were eating from the same cone. The picture told the whole story of lovebirds. They would take out a print from a shop and Sanjana would write the letter, as Usha was almost illiterate, though she had learned to read and write Hindi but her handwriting was bad. Moreover, there was a risk if Vicky had a doubt on her.

The letter exploded like a bomb in the hands of Megha's father. He was trembling with fear, anger and anxiety when Megha's mother brought a glass of milk in morning breakfast. The Megha's mother took the letter from his hands and read. She was disturbed, but did not lose her mental balance. She told her husband that she had full confidence in her daughter, and she would never take any step that could bring the disgrace to the family. She was sure that it was a conspiracy to defame their daughter, as she was very strict with the boys. She also pointed out that these days it was very easy to make a fake photograph with the help of computers.

All these arguments brought his anger down. He also trusted his daughter. He was convinced that a college student who was not able to entice Megha has done this mischief. Both of them decided to go to the city and inquire about the matter.

Megha's father appointed his substitute to worship in the temple in his absence. The sudden appearance of her parents surprised Megha. When granny asked the reason, they explained that they have come to meet the family of prospective bridegroom for Megha. It was understandable. Megha was still doubtful, since she had taken a promise from her mother that she would not marry her before completion of her research. They said that the parents of the person lived in the city but he worked in a metropolitan city.

After lunch when everybody was taking a rest in his own way, Megha's mother took her in the backyard and sat on a swing. She directly asked who is the boy she is having an affair with? Megha was jolted, so that is the reason of their sudden appearance. The news had reached the village and up to her parents. She repented being careless to go to the theater with Vicky. Now she could do nothing to recoup the damage. Megha said she met many class fellows, colleagues and friends but she does not have an affair with any one of them. Her mother took out a blurred picture in which back and side face of the Vicky was visible, and Megha was sharing ice cream with him.

Megha's fear had come true. That was the only day when she was with Vicky alone at a public place. There was no use denying the facts now. She still wants to do some face saving, so she said that she went to see a movie with her friends where Vicky had also come with his friends and since they did not have enough money everybody had to choose a partner to share the ice cream. However, it was a lame excuse but she knew even if the heart knows the truth, the mind wants to believe a lame excuse.

When Megha went to her room inside and her father came to join her mother. Her mother repeated the story, but father did not believe it. He found lots of the lacunas in the story. They were convinced that their daughter was having an affair with Vicky, who was of other caste and did menial job in a mall. They could not ask their daughter to drop her studies at this stage when she was almost half through her thesis. If they take her to their village, there was no library for reference books, and guide lived in the city.

The first thing Megha did when she reached her room was deleting all call detail history and sms history from her mobile. She sent last sms to the Vicky stating arrival of her parents and declined him to send sms or call. When she was just finished, her mother came to the room and asked for her mobile. She said her father wanted to check. She gave her mobile to mother and prayed that Vicky does not call for confirmation. No call or sms came that day. The next day Shalini called which was received by Megha's mother since now mobile was in her possession. She made an excuse that Megha would not go to college with her.

Megha could not imagine this happening with her. Her self-esteem was shaken and she once again cursed the day when she went to the theater with Vicky. She tried to remember all the faces in the theater; she could not recollect anyone she knew. Even if some casual acquaintance would see her, why would he report the matter to her parents, and that too with a picture? There is definitely sworn enemy who is not happy with her happiness. It could not be a boy since she was never close to any one of them. She maintained a distance and boys accepted her as a scholarly genius and respected her for that. She was soft-spoken and helpful girl. Who is the person who made a complaint to her parents? That was the million-dollar question.

Vicky was surprised when he read Megha's sms. No contact means no contact at any cost. There is something terribly wrong. Why her parents have come? They almost never leave the village unless there is some emergency. If the things were normal, she would say do not contact me I will contact you. Her message is loud and clear, there is some emergency. The more he thought about it the more anxious he became.

One week passed, he could concentrate neither on his work nor on his studies. Next Monday he received a call from Shalini.

"Will you go to the library today?" she inquired.

He had not made up his mind so far. However, it seems to be an invitation. Therefore, he consented.

"OK, meet me same place same time where you met Megha." He could never understand girls. Why do they exchange so much information with each other? What could be secret between two girls?, the phone was switched off before he could reply.

He reached in time and found Shalini standing under the same Neem tree opposite central library at sharp 11.00 AM. She looked pretty in her half ponytail shoulder cut hair spread on her back. She wore tight denim jeans and light olive green T-shirt. She was pretending to browse on her mobile, though she had seen him coming near to her. She could feel that this man is totally lost without his beloved. Her heart filled with sympathy for him. She had called him here to see his reaction. He had lots of sweet memories associated with this place.
"What happened with Megha?" his anxiety was apparent.

"Her parents have come to know about your affairs. They have your picture with her".

He was afraid of this from the beginning, more for Megha than for himself. She was too delicate to suffer such humiliation. That was the reason he preferred to meet her at a forlorn place where even if somebody known saw them would guess they are discussing books. This was true also. He was more anxious about the picture.

"What is in the picture?" he asked with apprehension.

"Both of you are eating ice-cream from the same cone at a crowded place" she informed.

"That must be the theater," Vicky guessed loudly.

"Yes, Megha is also of the same opinion. She repents that she forced you to take her to a movie" Shalini took her friend's favour.

"It is not her fault. I should not have agreed. Moreover, it was the destiny of all lovers, their parents come to know and time takes a test."

"What I should say to her," Shalini asked.

Vicky asked her everything and suggested that she should stick to her story that she was not alone with him but a group of friends had gone to watch a movie. Shalini asked about his studies and Vicky thanked her once again for providing the books. She said only thanks would not be enough he would have to offer coffee at Coasters whenever she could come with her friend, Megha. After that, Shalini went back to her home and Vicky entered the library. Vicky seriously pondered to find the offender who had complained against them. Hundreds of people from his village had settled in the city and many more came for a short visit to buy or sell the goods. Any one of them would do it especially if he was from their own community. Vicky had no intention to keep any grudge against complainant. It was more for the reason of curiosity than for revenge that he was searching for the culprit.

The more he thought about it, the more he got confused, so he stopped thinking about it. Within a few days, everything would be normal again. That is the beauty of time; it heals all types of wounds and restores normal life. He came to know through his messenger Shalini that the father of Megha had returned to town and the mother would stay with Megha until she completes her thesis. They would actively search for a suitable match for her. Her mobile would remain in the custody of her mother until she is satisfied that she has no stalker.

The messenger talked to the point, at the most, she would ask about his studies. Mostly Vicky also gave one word answers to her questions. One day after delivering a written message of Megha, she asked what was he reading these days. He told her that he was reading pastoral elegy "Adonais" written by Shelley when his friend Keats died. Shalini offered to recite a verse from Adonais and started humming.

The one remains, the many change and pass;
Heaven's light forever shines, Earth's shadow fly;
Life like a dome of many-coloured glass,
Stains the white radiance of Eternity,
Until Death tramples it to fragments.---Die.

Vicky explained that verse is theosophical, which searches, answers to some fundamental questions such as the origin and destiny of the human race and believes that there is one self-existent life from which all forms of life sprung.

Shalini had heard that Vicky was "well read" person and it was not possible to subjugate him as far as knowledge was concerned.

Shalini was good in cramming verses and her voice was melodious. It was fun for Vicky to hear her recite. Whenever she brought a message, he would ask her to recite a poem. She had never met anyone like Vicky. His enthusiasm for literature was unparalleled. Sometimes he would explain the hidden meaning of poetry or some interesting inside story, fact or biography of the author that helped in understanding the work of the poet.

Shalini was a resident of the city and had many friends and relatives. If they saw her with Vicky, they would not mind. In the city people avoided interfering in the personal life of other people. That is one major difference between urban and rural life. This and casteism draw a line of segregation.

Casteism is worse than communalism and racism. There could be some rationalization for communalism and racism but there was absolutely no reason to segregate society because of the caste. May be in primitive society it had some logic when caste were not determined by birth but by type of profession one chose depending upon his mental abilities, aptitude and temperament. However, the present structure of Hindu society where caste is such a dominating factor is abhorable.

Nothing sustains in the society without motivation. The motivation behind casteism is a political system. In a huge democratic country, all elections are fought and won and leaders are elected only on the basis of caste. We are ripe for our own "Age of reason".

Days tumbled into weeks and weeks into months. Vicky could not meet Megha, and her messenger Shalini became busy in her final year examination. Kiran had taken up her new job at Infosys seriously. It was the first time she found a platform for her creativity and earned appreciation from her peers and supervisors. May be that filled her emptiness to some extent.

Vicky also took his examination of previous year seriously and performed exceptionally well. Megha was afraid her parents may marry her before completion of her thesis if they found a proper match, so she began to work on her thesis. The topic of her thesis was "Shakti and Its Manifestation in Vedas" and her guide was a renowned scholar of Sanskrit, who had now, become Vice –Chancellor of National Sanskrit University. He was very busy with his new assignment but he would spare time for her whenever she sought his guidance. Megha told all this to Vicky when they were meeting outside library. She was on to concluding part of her thesis.

Examinations of previous and final year of English Literature were finished almost simultaneously. Vicky sent a message to Shalini that he wants to return her books and fixed up to meet at the library. He brought all her books and Shalini without his asking for it had brought final year's books. He teased "How do you know both of us would pass the examination? You could be sure about yourself but how do you know about me? "I know, both of us would clear the exams with flying colours." She retorted.

Both of them laughed and exchanged the books.

Shalini gave him full details of Megha's endeavours along with her message. The message was sent in the form of Sanskrit poetry which meant that a bereaved damsel is feeling a change in heart with the change of season. The poem was very disturbing for Vicky and he was upset. Shalini told him that parents of Megha do not want to linger and are actively searching a suitable match for her. Vicky asked if they will take the consent of Megha, Shalini from her own experience replied that parents of the girl take a formal consent if they are convinced that the proposal is best suitable for their girl.

Vicky asked Shalini what is the conclusion of Megha's research, she said whatever little she knows it establishes the supremacy of Adi-Parashakti and her various manifestations. Vicky wanted to know the details but Shalini was unable to tell him anything more than this. Since Vicky had received books of final year, he started his course studies. The syllabus of final year suited to his taste more and he was quite eager to master some of the new writers and poets.

The visits of Usha to the mall had become infrequent and he had not seen her for many days. On the day of his weekly off, he visited her house one afternoon. She was in her washroom and her younger brother was taking care of two children. He set down on the bed in a relaxed position when a mobile attached to charger chimed. He got up to see who was calling Usha. The screen displayed the name of Sanjana. The ringing stopped. Just because Vicky was idle and privacy was no issue with town people, he went to the gallery of her mobile and saw pictures. While going through the gallery he saw the picture in which he was standing with Megha in the lounge of the theater. He was stunned, his heartbeat stopped and his hand started shaking. His whole body shivered for a moment as if to neutralize high velocity of anger waves. At that moment, Usha came out naked from the washroom. She too was stunned to see Vicky with her mobile in his hands and knew its implication.

Whenever Usha used hair remover to remove hair from her private parts, she also used to shampoo her hair and put a face mask. This was her complete beauty treatment. She knew her brother and children are in another room and the washroom was attached to her bedroom so she had come out naked in haste to find out who the caller was.

When she saw a furious expression of Vicky holding her mobile all blood from her face drained. She became yellow with fear and guilt. Vicky in his anger had a tremendous desire to take Usha when he saw her naked, water dripping from her body, long hair soaked in water spread on her back and few locks hanging loose on her breast accentuating their beauty. He took her violently sparing nothing to the imagination.

What Vicky gave as punishment, Usha accepted as a reward.

Afterwards he left her house without speaking a single word with Usha. Now he knew that Usha took that picture in the theater and Sanjana had written that letter to the parents of Megha. The riddle was solved, that had bothered him for long.

Kiran took leave from Infosys to visit her parents in the town. She heard rumors of an affair between Vicky and Megha and went to meet Megha's mother. Megha's mother was a simpleton lady who admitted that she received a picture of Megha and Vicky and a letter about their affairs. She had heard that Usha had managed a fake picture and her friend Sanjana had written the letter. Why they would damage the reputation of their daughter was beyond comprehension of that noble woman. The whole town knew that Usha and Sanjana did not have 'good character' while Megha was quoted as an example of 'good character'.

Kiran was in touch with Vicky but he never told her about Megha. Kiran knew he took off on Monday, so she reached to his room in the city. Vicky was taking lunch. He had cooked Dal-Bati, which was popular cuisine of his province. Kiran had taken her breakfast at home before departing for city by bus. When Vicky offered her she also sat down to eat with him. The food was delicious and company of Vicky was nourishing. She felt a fulfillment. After they finished eating Kiran washed the dishes and Vicky helped her. Kiran realized he was the only man with whom she felt comfortable. By any chance, if it could be defined as love, she was in love with him.

When they settled on the single mattress, Kiran told Vicky everything about her life in Bangalore. About her room partner, food given in the mess, her colleagues, her boss, campus of Infosys, what she did on holidays, project she was working on, amenities on the campus, the cool ambience of the city and her favorite restaurants. She talked non-stop for about an hour while Vicky nodded his head occasionally, gruntled , raised his brows in fake surprise and murmured appreciatively. That is all they need to continue.

Then she asked how was his life and he said nothing new has happened. Kiran congratulated him for completing the first year of post graduation and asked about his studies. Both of them remained silent for sometime as if they knew that it was a silence before the storm.

Kiran Said "In the town people are talking about you and Megha"?

"So, what can I do?" Vicky remained evasive.

"You can at least tell me , if it is true or not?" Kiran persisted.

"Suppose it is true then?" Vicky was ready to hurt her due to his own guilt.

"Once again I would have reason to suicide" Kiran was desperate.

Vicky stared at the empty cocoon lying in the box on the shelf. Kiran had never noticed it before. She went up to the shelf and picked it up. She opened the little box and saw an empty cocoon.

"Why you have kept the empty cocoon like a precious diamond," Kiran asked.

"Because it is a precious diamond for me," Vicky endorsed her views.

"Who gave it to you"

"I can't tell"

"I have told you everything about my life", Kiran reminded him.

"That is your choice, Kiran, I never asked you. If you think what people are talking about me is correct, believe them. Don't ask me." Vicky gave a curt reply.

Kiran was sitting on the mattress with a bent in the knees and arms around them, puts her head on knees and sobs. Slowly the sobs became uncontrollable followed by hiccups and a wailing sound. Vicky got up unwillingly and brought a glass of water for her. She did not raise her head. Vicky asked her to drink water in a commanding voice. She accepted the glass and took a few small gulps.

"Kiran, don't cry", Vicky put his hand on Kiran's shoulder and withdrew; "I have never made any commitment to you. Why do you take me for granted?"

Kiran looked up, her eyes were swollen and pinkish in colour and some teardrops were still sticking to her curled up eyelashes. Her voice was almost like shriek due to stress, "why did you accept me again when I had rejected you and our relationship was over. Anyone would think that you have forgiven my past and ready to accept me as I am."

Vicky never expected that his help and sympathy would be taken as acceptance of a relationship and commitment. His feelings were never same for Kiran and Megha. Kiran left him emptier and life looked more absurd after each time they met. Megha fulfilled the vacuum of his life and he started searching the meaning of life when she was with him. However, he had not committed himself to anyone of them and took only that much liberty which they willingly offered.

Kiran got up from the mattress, washed her face with water in balcony and dried her face with a towel hung on a wooden peg. She saw her face in a small piece of mirror lying on the shelf. She loosened her braid and combed her hair. Her hairs were long up to the waist, jet black and lustrous. Such shiny healthy hair were weakness of Vicky. He always thought that thick bouncy hairs were indications of healthy sexual appetite.

Hairs were falling on both the sides of Kiran's face and some curly locks were still hanging loose on her forehead. Vicky could not resist the temptation to touch her hair. He combed her hair with his fingers, Kiran shivered, caught his hands and brought it to her lips and kissed on the back of his palm. He then brought her hands to his lips and kissed.

While departing she asked him in a very polite voice as if seeking his mercy.

"I need something from you" Kiran looked into his eyes.

Vicky trembled from inside when he saw how hollow her eyes were.

"If it is possible, I would not say no", Vicky assured her.

"Give me your box of empty cocoon, your precious diamond. I assure you I would return it to you if I decide to marry someone else." Kiran said.

"Only in that case", Vicky knew it was time to pass on the emptiness.

"No, even if I think about somebody else in my dreams, I would return it to you." The horizon of deserts loomed in the eyes of Kiran.

Vicky trusted her. Her emptiness and its eternity made her entitled for the gift she absolutely deserved. Vicky opened the small wooden box and looked at empty cocoon for a long time before he closed the lid and handed the box to Kiran.

Kiran touched it to her eyes as if it is gift of God and then softly kissed it.

She thanked Vicky before departing.

Next Monday Vicky got up late in the morning.

Vicky looked at his digital wristwatch. He was late by two hours for going to the library. He had an appointment with Shalini. She would bring her notes that she had prepared for final year. Vicky never read from notes. He had his own concept of what was important for him. But she insisted that her notes on "Literary Theory" were exceptionally very well written and she would also provide a reference book "A Handbook of Critical Approaches to Literature" by Wilfred L. Guerin. She knew the weakness of Vicky that he would never say no for a highly acclaimed reference book, which he could not afford to buy. Moreover, he always preferred to read from a book and never from photocopies or eBooks.

When Vicky reached library he found the Scooty of Shalini parked at stand. It meant she was still in the library. He found her sitting exactly the same place where Megha use to sit. He felt disturbed. All that is a good should never end. Good memories are more painful to live with than bad memories. Oh God, do not give me any good memories that pierce my heart to lament like a young widow.

As if Shalini could read his mind, she got up from the chair and left the library. Vicky followed her. She went straight under a Neem tree where he used to meet Megha. Either she was teasing him or she wants to heal his mind by reconditioning he could not guess. She took out notes and reference book and handed them over to him. Shalini told him that Kiran had come to meet Megha and they have talked about him. Megha was not good at hiding the truth, so she has told everything about their relationship and cried. While consoling her, Kiran also started crying and both of them cried together. A small wooden box was exchanged between them all the time when they were crying.

"Do you know about that wooden box?" Shalini asked.

"Yes, I have gifted it to Kiran",Vicky replied.

"What is in it?" Shalini inquired.

"You should better ask your friends".

Shalini remained silent after that. Vicky felt bad for giving a curt reply. He presumed that she knows about the empty cocoon, but wants to hear the story from his angle. He was too upset after the visit of Kiran. He asked Shalini to arrange a meeting with Megha as he wanted to discuss the visit of Kiran with her. Shalini assured him that she would try her best to arrange a meeting at the earliest possible.

Shalini informed him that she had enrolled herself for M.Phil. and he should suggest her some topic for dissertation. Vicky suggested she should work on deconstruction theories which is serious topic

rather than common and popular topics like Romanticism.
Kiran left on her scooty and Vicky walked towards the bus stand as usual.

Vicky went to the house of Usha next Monday. He gave her Rs.1500/- that he had borrowed from her so far. Vicky decided to severe all relations with Usha, since she had ditched him. His anger against her was still not subsided. He felt no grudge against her friend Sanjana with whom he had met only once. She had acted on the stance of Usha and had become neutral towards him after watching his standard of living. Even that did not matter to him; he knew that most of the girls were like that. The sole culprit of ruining his life was Usha. He would return her money, so that she has no reason to intervene in his life.

There was a crowd assembled outside the house of Usha. He hurried toward her home and made his way inside, where on a bed brother of Usha was lying and neighbours consoled Usha. When Usha saw him, she got up from the side of the bed and started crying. Vicky was told that her brother Sona Ram has been suffering from fever for last three days and had fits of convulsions about an hour back and lost his consciousness. Usha had immediately called the neighbours and one of them took out his shoes and brought it near his nose. After a few minutes the convulsions stopped but Sona Ram was unconscious. They were thinking of calling a doctor when Vicky reached.

First of all he requested neighbours to vacate the room so that patients can have fresh air. The teeth of Sona Ram were still clenched so he opened the jaw by force and inserted a spoon so that his tongue is not damaged. He washed the face of Sona Ram with a towel soaked in cold water. Sona Ram regained his consciousness and asked for water to drink. Due to a seizure he was weak and his voice was still not clear.

Vicky then took Usha and Sona Ram to a nearby hospital. The physician prescribed some medicines and tests. Vicky bought the medicines but Usha refused to test, she said she would consult her husband first. Bhola also reached the hospital directly and the doctor asked them to calm down. He said there could be many reasons for seizures and it would take some time to cure the disease.

Usha told the doctor that after seizures were over Sona Ram was talking many irrelevant things and when she tried to stop him, he attacked her. He had become very violent and even two neghbours had to hold him by force to stop from attacking Usha. Sona Ram had even bitten on the wrist of one neighbor who was holding him. During that time, Sona Ram did not recognize anybody.

Doctor had a medical explanation for amnesia, which only Vicky could understand. When they came out of hospital, Usha told Bhola that Sona Ram had gone out a few days back at noon after taking milk and had also stepped inadvertently on a totka on the crossroads. When he came back, he had a fever since then. Bhola also had a strong faith in evil spirits, so they decided to take Sona Ram to the temple of Hanuman in the village where a Bhopa was famous for curing such supernatural ailments.

They asked Vicky to accompany them next Monday. Vicky advised that they should take medical tests and medicines prescribed by the doctor. Usha and Bhola were of the view that such diseases are not cured by medicines and it would be a sheer wastage to spend money on tests. They decided to visit the temple for cure.

The temple of Mehndipur Balaji Is located on national highway from Jaipur to Delhi. It has international reputation for cure of supernatural ailments caused by evil spirits. This temple is always crowded with devotees who have come to pay homage after cure or they are family members of the patient. Patients were shaking their heads violently in the huge campus of the temple and shouting obscenities loudly. Relatives were restraining patients by holding them by force. The chief priest performed the rituals and talked to the evil spirit directly. He was holding a young woman by her hair and smoke of red chilies, black pepper, mustard, and clove was in the air. The woman was trying to liberate herself from the clutches of the chief priest and was abusing profusely. These kinds of obscenities are not expected from a young woman.

"Who are you?" priest asked.

"I am Kan Singh" woman replied in a coarse manly voice.

"Why are you in her body" priest shouted.

"She pissed under the tree, I was sleeping on" woman replied.

"So what, can't she piss when she feels like? How would she know you are there?" priest was still shouting. He shook her head by hair to torture the spirit.

"It is a rule to cough to warn us when you piss in open under trees. Moreover, she menstruated after urinating. I had to leave that tree where I lived for many years, so I entered her body" evil spirit replied through woman in an angry voice.

"O.K., you have taken your revenge, now leave her body and go back to tree." Priest commanded.

"'No, I like the body of this girl. She uses very good perfumes that I love so much. I won't leave her." Evil spirit protested.

The eyes of the priest turned red in anger. He took water from his vase and sprinkled it on the young woman. The woman tried to run away but her relatives were holding her with force that she could not move.

The Priest again took water from a vase sprinkled it while reciting mantra. The woman became extremely violent and priest beat her with a peacock feather broom. The woman cried in male voice, "Don't beat me"

Priest threatened, "I will put you in a bottle and seal it, and you would never come out of it".

This threatening worked and woman apologized in thick male voice and sought pardon of the priest. The Priest ordered the spirit of Kan Singh to leave her body immediately and never come back.

The woman fainted after this for a while and when she regained her consciousness, she behaved like a normal woman.

When Sona Ram was brought before the priest, the priest talked with him. Priest declared that there was absolutely no evil spirit in Sona Ram and they should consult a doctor. Still for their satisfaction, he gave ajhada by touching him with a peacock feather broom from head to toe three times along with mantra recitation.

Vicky realized that many patients genuinely suffered from evil spirits, while others were patients of schizophrenia, anxiety, hysteria and other nervous system disorders like epilepsy, meningitis, eclampsia and psychopathic ailments.

Ignorance breeds faith. When medical science fails to cure an ailment even learned people go in the shelter of miracle cures based on black magic, superstitions and charisma. The campus was crowded with a mixed crowed of rich and poor, literate, illiterate, rural, urban, male and females of all age groups.

Now Usha had no argument against medical tests and treatment. Vicky spent all his money when they went to Mehandipur Balaji and later on tests and medicines. He never asked for money from Usha or Bhola ,nor kept an account of money spent by him. Usha saw a different Vicky, who had not only forgiven her blunder but also helped her in a crisis. Now she realized how mean she was and how magnanimous Vicky was. She felt guilty of her behavior and resolved to apologize in private. She had sweet memories of the day when Vicky had aggressively taken her filling her all the space that emptiness had caused by the curse of the cat that lived in the empty dry well of the village.

The well was inverted and hung over her, and her own existence was reduced to the little brown cat who dwelled on the rim of well that constituted her two worlds. It was more complicated than this. The Cat had remained a silent observer of her first encounter with Mohan Singh from the tree under which she lost her virginity. In between all those years of her first encounter and taken by Vicky aggressively her soul was constantly tormented by little brown cat, whom she had disturbed by causing echo in the well. The revenge of the cat was over and she had left her body. The weight of inverted well was removed from over her and she felt like a bird set free from the cage.

After medical tests prescribed by a doctor it was established that Sonaram suffered from a parasitic infection known as cysticercosis. It was initial stage, the worm had just reached the brain. Bhola and his family were vegetarian so worm reached to the body of Sona Ram by unwashed cabbage and spinach eaten raw by Sona Ram. That could be true because Sona Ram was fond of eating raw salad sometimes unwashed or not properly washed.

Doctor assured that the parasite would die by medication. Usha did not trust medical science when doctors talked in the language of probability. If the larva of the parasite has formed a cyst, it may not die easily with medication, and in that case, the doctor would have to operate which could even be fatal. Usha was very affectionate to her younger brother and her concern for his health touched Bholaram, who once thought that Usha has financial motives in providing boarding to her brother.

Usha came to know that a Sadhu in Mathura is an expert in taking out worm from the brain. The Manager refused holidays to two of his employees, so it was settled that Vicky would accompany Usha and Sona Ram to Mathura.

The Sadhu was actually a married man who lived a simple married life. His Guru in Himalaya taught the cure to him. He used herbal powder by the smell of which the larva came out with a sneeze. Vicky was surprised to see such a simple cure of a complicated disease. The Sadhu did not charge any money for this. Out of his own sweet will, Vicky paid him one hundred rupee note.

Shalini always conveyed the message to Megha that Vicky wants to meet her but never encouraged her to do so. She knew that due to their traditional family background, they would not be able to marry and further intimacy would only complicate the matter. Though she knew in her heart that Megha and Vicky made an ideal couple physically and mentally but due to their background they were not made for each other.

Megha had introduced Kiran to Shalini. Kiran, Shalini and Vicky were of the same caste. Shalini had told Megha that she should not dream to marry Vicky and they should only plan to spend some great time together, before destiny pulls them apart. This theory finally settled into the mind of Megha and she promised she would not involve herself emotionally too much with Vicky.

She asked Shalini to arrange their meeting. Shalini recited a verse of Urdu poetry by Mirza Galib which meant the fire was equally intense on both the sides.

The old English proverb "Where there is will there is a way" proved to be right once again. The guide of Megha who had become a Vice –Chancellor in a Sanskrit University, came to preside the seminar organized by "Pandit Madhusudan Ojha Research Foundation" on "Psychology in Vedas". He was an authority on Carl Jung's work based on a study of the Mandala , when he visited India. Due to his diversion to occult Jung was more popular for mystic work rather than as scientific psychoanalyst.

He had called Megha to attend the seminar and also show him her concluding chapter. Megha was enormously happy that God had heard her prayers and once her guide approved the conclusion her thesis would be completed in time. She had already sent the concluding chapter to her guide by email. She talked to her granny and got permission to attend seminar and consult the guide afterwards.

She reached to the seminar and occupied a back seat since her senior colleagues and academicians were also invited. The chair next to her was vacant and she was busy watching the dais when a voice startled her

"May I" Vicky was seeking her permission to sit next to her.

"By all means" she replied in a weak voice.

A lump reached up to her throat and she could listen to her own heartbeat.

"How come you are here?" she inquired.

"I was invited, I am a lifetime member of the foundation" he replied.

What else you can expect from a scholar. The Seminar was to continue up to late afternoon. The foundation arranged the working lunch. They had three hours if they wanted to spend together. Therefore, Vicky got up and left the conference hall. He stood outside where drinking water was available in containers. He drank water, meanwhile Megha also joined. He asked her to come with him. She followed; he hired a taxi for his room. Within a few minutes, they were in the privacy of his room.

They embraced tightly kissing fervently each other all over the face. The storm of passion engulfed both of them in. The multiple storm turned into the cyclone and when it was over it was as soothing as a sunny day in the winters.

They did not want to remain absent from seminar for long and be noticed. They decided to reach back to the seminar hall separately. The less they were seen together the better it would be. Vicky sent her in auto taxi first and then followed by a city bus. They occupied chairs in the last row. The speech of the speaker did not register in their mind so they went out of the seminar hall many times that day. However, since they were sitting in the last row nobody noticed.

After Seminar Megha went up to her guide and touched her feet. He uttered a Sanskrit verse in blessings. They talked intimately like true Guru-chela and Megha looked very happy from the distance. While departing she again touched his feet and he gave her a slight hug in the farewell. When she came to Vicky she radiated high energy, her final chapter had been approved by her guide and he had sent her an email just before coming to the seminar.

He had talked with Head of the Department in Sanskrit Language and she should deposit the bind thesis in three copies at the earliest possible. Shortly she would get a call for Viva-Voce.

"This needs a celebration", Vicky demanded without any hope.

"Of course, let's go back" Megha consented.

That was a windfall gain. Lovers are greedy persons.

Before departing, they planned to have coffee in Coasters. It was dangerous to be seen together in the café lest somebody informs her parents, Megha invited Shalini on the mobile of Vicky. When they were sipping coffee, Vicky thanked Shalini for informing him that Megha was attending the seminar.

Megha did not know whether to curse her friend for being a traitor or thank her for the nice time she could spend with Vicky.

Granny had already talked with relatives to suggest a suitable boy for Megha. She was pleased to know that Megha would submit her thesis soon to get degree of doctorate. The education level in Brahmins was high and she was sure that she would find a scholar match for her. When Megha told that she would need her laptop back to check mail from the guide and seek day-to-day guidance for finalization of thesis, granny willingly gave her laptop back.

Once she made the necessary correction suggested by her guide the thesis was ready for final print. Again she sought granny's permission to go out to get the prints. Megha looked very innocent to granny and her heart was not ready to believe that she had any affair with any boy. The restrictions imposed by Megha's parents were very unnatural in the modern age. She had a belief "trust your children even if they are not worthy of it", Megha in her opinion was trustworthy.

Megha chose Monday to go out for print. She took the whole thesis in her pen drive and went to the shop, which was famous for best quality work in the thesis. He handed him her pen drive and gave instructions. He offered to collect the books after three hours. She had already informed Vicky by sms on the laptop. When she reached, Vicky was waiting for her in his best clothes, clean shaved and well combed hair. The mild smell of musk-filled the room that could be either his after shave lotion or a deodorant. When he would embrace, she would know.

Vicky was more poised and balanced today. He had made up his mind to be slow and steady. Megha saw he was serving her favourite Pizza from Mac Donald in two dishes. He had also brought a pouch of coffee milk was already on slow mode of the stove. He took the coffee powder in a cup, added sugar and a spoon of milk. He stirred it vigorously. Soon the coffee was frothing; he divided into two cups and poured milk.

They ate Pizza and sipped coffee.

When she reached home, her granny was waiting for her in the drawing room. Her heart skipped a beat. Granny affectionately called her to sit near her on the sofa. Megha took out bound copies of her thesis, and gave them in the hands of granny. Granny was extremely pleased and blessed her. Then she took out an envelope from under the cushion and handed her. When Megha opened it, it had a postcard size photograph of a young handsome man and a sheet of his biodata. Her eyes became moist and she hide her face in the lap of granny to conceal her tears. It is customary for a girl to shy when elders talk about her marriage.

Settled on a couch, in the privacy of her room, Megha looked at the photo. His name was Dr. Prashant Sharma and he was lecturer of Philosophy in the central university of the province at the capital. He looked handsome and elegant. His hairs were long and curled up at back like characters of the ancient era, the golden frame of spectacles enhanced his wisdom and authority. His age, qualification and family background was a perfect match with Megha.

Granny arranged a meeting of parents from both the sides. When parents were satisfied Prashant and Megha were allowed to converse in private. They talked about their research topic, and by the time, they wanted to switch the topic they were called back. They gave their consent and the ceremony of engagement was performed very day.

The gap between engagement and marriage is romantic, adventurous, fluttering but dangerous also. Due to frequent means of communications, excessive information is exchanged between two so far strangers, which may lead to misunderstanding and sometimes a breakup. The journey of the trust that has just begun is derailed, because one was stupid enough to share information about weaker moments of life.

Every person by the time he or she reaches to reasonable age of marriage have come across an incident of heartthrob, soft corner, love affair, one night stand or a live together. When the life has taken a blind turn and if you look back there is nothing to see, it is not good to recapitulate.

Megha trod the path carefully. She never mentioned the name of Vicky, stopped sending messages through Shalini, and never met him after her engagement.

On the other hand Vikcy grew impatient, he never expected such a callous behavior from Megha.

Who one day is yours at your whims and mercy to enjoy it in whatever way you want, may other day be of someone else.

This realization takes time to precipitate. One should be careful in choosing what one wants to possess, and when you start discarding things that you cannot possess forever you come to know that there is nothing to possess.

Kiran came from Bangalore to attend the marriage. Vicky did not go to attend the marriage, though his parents came from the town to attend marriage and gave an ornament of gold since it is auspicious to gift gold in the marriage of a priest's daughter. Kiran stayed in Megha's house where Shalini also joined them. They talked about everything under the sun but none uttered the name of Vicky even once.

When Megha was sent off after the wedding, Kiran went to meet Vicky. She carried the small wooden box containing empty cocoon. Vicky looked at her when she returned the box. After Megha's marriage this was second shock to him. Kiran said she has not met anyone so far but she thinks she has no right to carry the part of his existence with her. If Vicky would have given it willingly, on his own she could have made his emptiness as part of her own existence. Moreover, it emitted lots of negative energy in her room and her room partner was uncomfortable with it.

Vicky was not interested in her explanation. Only the end matters. He accepted and placed it at the same place on the shelf. Kiran informed him that she met Mohan when she went to town. Vicky asked, is that why she is returning the box? Kiran looked hurt. Vicky felt ashamed for asking such a stupid question. Kiran said Mohan is suffering from some fatal sickness. He has lost his weight and looks like Skelton. Rumor is that he suffers from AIDS. Everybody was acquainted with sexual vagaries of Mohan and had little sympathy for his sufferings.

Mohan was the first love of Kiran.

People usually have sweet memories of their first crush, even if it ends in a break up.

What happened to Kiran was not ordinary break up; it was a worst nightmare of her life. She could never recollect any sweet memories of the time spent with Mohan. Kiran's mother was sure that Mohan is terminally sick due to her curse. KIran was neutral, neither she was happy nor sad. She met him accidentlly when she went to the temple. The parents of Mohan were performing "Mahamritunjay Yajna" for recovery of Mohan. When she came out of sanctum Sanctorum, Mohan stood before her with folded hands. His hollow eyes were sunk in the high forehead and cheekbones. He had covered himself with black woolen shawl since he always suffered from fever. Once he looked so very handsome in black shawl that girls waited for winters to see him wrapped up in this shawl.

He said " Kiran I am sorry, please forgive me if possible"

Kiran said nothing, just looked at him in his eyes once and left. There was no forgiveness in her eyes.

If you are young, powerful, rich and handsome, you may think that you can conquer the world. The power makes you blind and you hurt the people while seeking enjoyment. Sex is not sin; abusing sexual power is a sin. If nobody is hurt or pleased, it is a mere animal act performed by natural instincts granted by God for progenration.

Kiran narrated the whole incident without any emotion. She could not even hate Mohan. She said she does not blame Mohan alone, her friend Kirti and her fiancé Sunder were also involved in the conspiracy. Moreover, she admitted her fault for choosing the wrong type of persons as friend.

She blamed Vicky for not challenging her divorce case in "Gram Panchayat". They would have definitely rejected the application of Kiran, since no divorce is granted on the ground of education.

Vicky did not protest since he did not believe in child marriages and an educated girl had a right to choose her own life partner.

"Do you know, how does it feel when you know that you would die soon?" Kiran asked suddenly.

"How can I know, nor I want to know. For me each day is a gift of God" Vicky said.

Kiran knew Vicky also had the same neutral feeling for Mohan. While departing she told him that in the marriage of Megha, Shalini was all the time talking about him. She said this to see how he reacts. Vicky said she has helped him in his post graduation. There was no expression on his face, but Kiran felt some vibrations. She had observed that during the marriage ceremony, Shalini was taking special care of the parents of Vicky, and they had liked her. Girls of marriageable age are more far-sighted than young girls who are emotional.

Next Monday when he was getting ready to go to the library, he received a call from Shalini. She invited him at her home for lunch. She wanted to discuss her dissertation topic with him. He could not find any excuse so he said yes. He reached at given time. Her parents received him. They talked about his parents back in town and that Kiran met them in marriage and found them noble. Her father was employee of Indian Railways and belonged to a village. The grandfather of Kiran was an agriculturist. Vicky felt more comfortable with the people of rural background. Meanwhile Kiran brought tea and snacks. After tea, she took Vicky in her room. The room was neat, clean, and well decorated.

She had carefully selected the books to display, since she knew Vicky would hardly notice any other arrangements made by her.

Vicky stood frozen before the shelf of books. Each book was worth a read. The genre was wide and selection of the books was unparallel. Many of these books were in Vicky's wish list. Vicky took out some books randomly and tried to discuss with Shalini, but she made an excuse that she had recently bought the book and could not find time to read it. She might have purchased a few books to impress him but her choice was best, Vicky thought.

Then they settled on the sofa and prepared an outline of the dissertation. Shalini had done some homework and she had taken prints of many articles that she found on the internet. She had googled Darrida with a different set of words and found many valuable articles.

When they finished the work,the mother called her to bring Vicky for lunch. The food was delicious and was served with great affection by the mother of Shalini.

There were no city buses outside. A neighbor informed that all city bus owners had gone on strike after dispute with traffic police demanding heavy bribe. Shalini's mother asked Shalini to drop Vicky at his home on her scooty.

Vicky insisted he would walk; he was not habitual of driving a scooty that he thought was a ladies vehicle and he would feel awkward in sitting behind Shalini. Town people are more in the habit of walking in comparison to urban people who prefer to use two to four wheelers even for short distances.

In urban areas when people consult a physician for very common ailment like Blood Pressure, Diabetes, Obesity doctor says it is a life style disorder and they should go for morning walk. Even the morning walk of urban people is shorter than the average distance walked by rural people.

Vicky reclined on his second hand bamboo rocking chair, which he inherited from a colleague that was living city for good to work in metropolitan mall. The chair was best to read a book, devoid of any sternness that a new chair has. He brought cushions from the Mall to sit on and for backrest and made it cozy. Sometime he would doze off in the chair reading a book until late at night.

The slow rocks of chair helped him in concentrating on the issue. The question asked by Kiran still loomed in his mind though he had given a formal reply without thinking.

"Do you know, how does it feel when you know that you would die soon?"

Every person is born with a countdown, so it is only a matter of time, which is accurately measurable in nanoseconds or by a number of times, one will breathe in his lifetime. The Sages had a longer life span by controlled breathing techniques. Fear, Sleep, Food and Sex are the only Life Forces in all animals, and your degree of humanity depends on the degree of control you can exercise over these forces. All human being have a freedom either to give up to these forces and act like an animal or to control these forces and divert the energy in a positive direction. A choice come from impressions and education, to strengthen them or not is the first choice on which all other choices depend. With a strong conscience, one can be a master of the senses rather than a slave.

Impressions are subjective though the source is society, but education is entirely a function of society and when society fails to deliver its duties, why it should blame a person for making a wrong choice.

Mohan was brought up in a traditional Rajput family. He learned to smoke hukka in his early childhood. His grandfather taught him how to prepare hukka for smoking. When he brought a burning charcoal to put on tobacco leaves, his grandfather asked him to take a few puffs of hukka. As an adolescent, he had seen his father enjoying concubines and exploiting women of lower caste. He finished his schooling with flying colours due to the influence of his father. In fact he had little knowledge of any subject and could not locate even five countries on the world map.

Nobody could dare to make a complaint against Mohan to his father. Once complainant of lower caste was publicly whipped when he complained that his minor daughter was raped by Mohan. Mohan's father said that there is no dearth of girls for Mohan that he would rape a lower caste minor girl. The girl must be a whore who enticed a Rajput prince for pecuniary benefits, so get money for it. Mohan's father threw a few hundred-rupee notes on the face of the father, who collected the money and left. Not taking money would have further enraged the Thakur, Mohan's father.

Mohan was the Casanova of the town, as far as gambling and women were concerned. His charms were irresistible and he was an iconic macho man for the youth. If Kiran fell for him, it was not her fault.

Kiran was brought up in an atmosphere of discipline. The value system in trade caste is superior and they were considered as carriers of cultural values of the society. They were affluent but never did vulgar exhibition of the wealth. Kiran was intelligent in studies and she had performed well in the entrance examination of the Engineering College.

The long days of summer, her idle mind, boredom, anxiety of result, proximity of lovesick friend Kirti, led her to consent to meet Mohan. What started as little adventure to break the monotony of life ended in tragedy that changed the course of her life.

Once crochet, shuttle work, weaving, mending and embroidery were taught to the girls to keep their mind engaged in creativity. Those arts have become obsolete and soap operas are slowly poisoning the society with a modern value system.

Lost in his thought in the dim light of sunset he saw a vague structure of a wooden box with half-closed eyes. The weight of the emptiness created by cocoon was too heavy for Kiran. It is good that she has returned it. May be he should also return it to Usha. He had a feeling that after his aggressive encounter with Usha, she was relaxed and normal as if some evil spirit had left her body. That spirit brought Usha naked before his eyes exactly at the moment when he was holding her mobile with his picture with Megha in his hand, and his rage was never as much out of control, as on that day.

His mobile beeped. Kiran had called probably from Banglore. Her college was celebrating annual function and Kiran was very excited since she was performing a folk dance "Kalbeliya" that was favourite of Vicky. She invited Vicky in the function and took a promise from him that he would come. Vicky applied for one-week leave from mall and made reservations in train for Bangalore.

He stayed in the guest house of the company. The ambience was cool and it was good to see a lot of joyful ambitious youth. The performance of Kiran was highly applauded by the audience. Kiran was busy all the time so Vicky went to Hampi for a day and came back to his own city refreshed.

He felt a new surge of optimism after his Banglore visit and concentrated on his final year examination. Shalini was preparing for one year M.Phil and her examination for second semester were now due.In first semester she had opted "Indian writing in English" as special paper and in second semester she had opted "Colonial Discourse Theory" and "English in India". Their meetings in the library were regular, since Shalini would need to consult or borrow a book for a few days for reference. Their friendship was based on mutual respect, which is the backbone of all healthy and durable relationships.

When the examinations were, over he visited hometown after a long time. His friends and parents in the town were happy. They found Vicky has changed, he had become more disciplined and responsible. He visited the temple regularly to recite "Visnushastranaam". Megha had taught him to recite the correct pronunciation of Sanskrit words. He could not dare to ask the father of Megha about her. He prayed Vishnu to find a way.

The mother of Megha came to lunch at Vicky's home on the death anniversary of his grandmother. Vicky's mother after lunch donated a cow, sari with five clothes, silver anklet and some steel utensils. After lunch, both the women gossiped for some time exchanging family information.

Vicky overheard everything pretending to read a book. He came to know that University had awarded a doctorate to Megha. She was in the family way. Her husband was very nice and caring. Megha was enrolled as guest faculty in the University. Vicky felt a pang of jealousy and was immediately ashamed of it; Megha was his best friend and she deserved all the happiness.

The population of the town was about ten thousand and there were only ten families of the trade caste, constituting hardly fifty people. All families assembled on the festivals related to the deities of their clan. Vicky enjoyed this type of idiosyncrasies of a clan, carried from one generation to another for thousands of years. Since it was an important day for the family, the mother of Kiran also came to pay her homage to deceased soul. She was very fond of Vicky's grandmother and always sought her guidance in all family matters. She was sad and missed her since she wanted to seek guidance about Kiran. It was due to their good family relations, that Vicky's grandmother had accepted her proposal of Kiran for Vicky, even when they were children. If Kiran had not revolted, they would have still been relatives.

Kiran made a choice. She was prudent girl and had consistently excelled in academic career. She had ambition to become a successful Engineer. Vicky did not fit well in the picture of her future life, since he was rusticated from college on the charges of drug addiction. Moreover, she did not believe in a relationship thrust up on her just because her mother was under influence of Vicky's grandmother. She compelled her mother to apply for divorce in the Panchayat Court. Her mother visited the Vicky's house, apologized profusely for the conduct of her daughter, and took a promise from her grandmother that it would not affect the relation between two families adversely.

Vicky's parents decided not to protest against the petition and divorce was granted easily. Both the mothers were worried about future of their children.

Vicky's mother had already asked him about some marriage proposals pending with her. Vicky had requested to decline all proposals and give him two more years of freedom to make his career. His mother faltered and agreed.

Vicky went to meet Mohan Singh. He was still looking for an answer to Kiran's question. He had seen Mohan Singh as a robust courageous man, now to see him weak and timid was a shock to Vicky. The fear of death loomed in his eyes, but he pretended to be brave. He was bed ridden most of the time and went for a small walk in the evening. Mohan Singh told him that he wants to make a big school complex in town where the best education would be provided to the children by modern gadgets and no fees would be charged from poor families. He had donated his personal land for the purpose and an architect has prepared a master plan for the project. He had asked some renowned academicians to join the Board of Directors. He requested Vicky to join advisory committee and Vicky could not refuse to help in a noble cause, though he said he is not worthy of it. Mohan Singh had a very high opinion about him.

Object of death is to give a meaning to life. Those who see themselves closer to death every day, find a meaning of life. Thousands of people die every day, without any notice from death. Mohan Singh said he is lucky that God had sent him a notice so much in advance that he could plan his remaining life. Vicky had never cried in his life but a teardrop rolled down his cheeks in admiration of Mohan Singh.

He not only found the answer of Kiran's question, but also developed an insight into his own behavior guided by his sub-conscious mind. He had gone to Mohan Singh's house to express his sympathy, which was his way to make him look down and feel guilty about his past. Mohan Singh had snatched that opportunity from him.

Brave people deserve forgiveness. They take lessons from the defeat and fight back. They earn the respect of their enemies. Death and destiny are two most strong enemies of mankind, most of the people accept their defeat and recline, but there are very few like Mohan Singh, who dare to fight the destiny of death and win it over by immortal act.

Chief Minister of the state came in the foundation ceremony of educational institution. The photo gallery of the future projection of the education center was a major attraction. After school education, most of the youth in town preferred to have some vocational training in the trades. Mohan Singh had approached the recently retired Director of Technical Education, Indra Mohan Sharma who was a renowned educationist. He had agreed to work on the Board of Directors. He would take care of the Vocational training wing of the institution. He had proposed five trades initially, which were very popular in youth due to career opportunities. Mechanical, Electrical, Motor Winding, Carpentry and Computer Hardware Courses were job oriented due to the rapid growth of industrialization.

Besides this other course like School Teaching Certificate, Medical Paraphernalia courses, Physiotherapist and geriatrics nursing were also seen as a good opportunity to make a career. Due to availability of land, money, expert teachers from the city and Private Public Partnership Policy of the government, the institution had potential for expansion. The dream of Mohan Singh started taking a shape. Vicky received an official letter to send the consent for empanelment on the advisory committee.

Vicky always promoted vocational training after schooling. The graduation courses in arts or science were not job oriented and youth felt ashamed in doing menial jobs after higher education. This unemployed educated rural youth is a major segment of the society that is facing frustration. Vicky was also one of them.

He found that his job of a salesperson in a mall was derogatory and his quality of life will deteriorate until one day his existence would be reduced to an insect. He cannot imagine of marriage and family as desired by his mother in his present circumstances.

Due to the ample availability of skilled and unskilled labour in the town and enough stone mines in proximity, the construction work of the school was finished within one year, much ahead of the schedule. During this one year Vicky completed his post graduation and received a Gold Medal. Shalini completed her M.Phil. and got enrolled for degree of Ph.D. Kiran received an offer from the company for foreign assignment and she opted to work in the USA for three years. She left for Chicago from Indira Gandhi International Airport, New Delhi, and Vicky went to New Delhi to see her off.

Thankfully, she had returned the empty cocoon to him, with the weight of that empty well on her head she would have never taken that decision to go abroad. Only the shackle free souls get a chance to cross international boundaries. Kiran was excited about her assignment, as she would get an exposure by working with western counterparts. This would help in her carrier building.

Vicky already missed her when the plane took off. You know the value of people when they do not remain easily accessible to you. He was her only oasis in her otherwise emotionally barren life. He has no right to snatch that away from her until the caravan of her life reaches to destination.

At that time, the wooden box would also reach to its rightful hands.

Or, would take him to the grave!

That night Vicky saw the worst nightmare of his life. He had come back to his city directly from outside the aerodrum and reached to his room when it was getting dark. The darkness was slowly engulfing the city due to power cut. People who did not have inverters in their home kept chimneys ready for such occasions. Vicky was not in the mood to cook food so ate in a hotel. The hotel was famous with peasants. He cooked very thick chapattis, charged money per chapatti .The vegetable was very spicy, and red chili with a thick layer of oil was free with chapatti. People with very good appetite could not eat more than two chapattis. Vicky was hungry and tired due to long journey so he ate two.

He always preferred to spend some time in the rocking chair before he hits the mattress. He picked up "Nausea" and started reading it. He read it until past midnight. After that, he slowly dozed off. He tried to get up and reach up to the mattress but his legs could not bear the weight of his body and he stumbled upon the mattress in almost sleepy condition. He felt as if someone else had pushed him from rocking chair who found the chair occupied by unauthorized persons.

He heard some voices, that were familiar but he could not recollect, he could not even strain his mind to recollect. It turned into stranger's voice, which was hollow, without life and fearsome. He could feel his body shivered, his throat was dry and he was thirsty, but he could not muster the strength to get up and drink water. He wanted to shout for help but no voice came from his throat.

Then the source of voice started taking shape. First two shining eyes like tiny powerful bulbs became visible. It was a cat. His eyes were locked with the eyes of the cat. The cat looked at him with revengeful and vindictive stare. His whole body perspired profusely, he wanted to scare the cat by throwing something at her, but could not dare do so. The cat was holding something with teeth and sneered. She was holding cocoon and blood was dripping from it. The cat looked at him accusingly, as if he was responsible for the bloodshed. Then the cat jumped on his face and he shrieked with horror. He could feel her landing on his face and scratches of her claws on his throat and forehead. She was trying to suffocate him by pressure of her claws. He could not breathe. As if to save life, he caught her with both the hands and threw her in the balcony. The cat disappeared.

Now he could see the cocoon lying on his chest. The cat had left it there. It had some movements. As if something from inside wants to come out. The cocoon was as heavy as big boulder of rock. When it moved, his ribs cracked under the weight. He could not pick it up and throw. Then one end of the cocoon opened and a caterpillar walked out of it. His head was big in comparison to rest of his body. His two bulging eyes inspected the whole room and rested on Vicky's face. Except that he was heavy, he was not scary. Slowly his face turned into Mohan Singh and the rest of the body remained of caterpillar. Mohan Singh did not pretend any bravery; he was weeping and requesting to save his life. He did not want to die. He had seen nothing in his life; it is so cruel to die when young. He was sobbing uncontrollably and the shirt of Vicky was soaked with his tears. Vicky wanted to console but he had no words.

Slowly the face turned into caterpillar again. The wings grew on his sides, and it turned into a beautiful butterfly. For a few moments, it fluttered into the room, over the wooden box and then flew away through the balcony.

Vicky felt light and touched his chest where caterpillar was sitting. It was all wet. He woke up. His whole body was soaked with perspiration. His heart was still beating faster and throat dry. It was a great relief to find that the nightmare was over. The box was lying at its place. He got up and switched the light on. The power supply was restored. He drank a glass of water and recited Vishnusahstranaam sitting on a mattress. After that, he slept soundly for the rest of the night.

The next day when he reached the mall, Bhola told him that Mohan Singh had expired last night. In cases of death, the Manager was lenient. He allowed both of them to go. What type of social being a man would be if he does not spare time for his near and dear ones who have left this world? Many women fainted when the bereaved brother, father and two uncles of Mohan Singh lifted for cremation the dead body of Mohan Singh tied to bamboo bed and covered with white cloth on shoulders. There cannot be a bigger curse for a father than this? It was a very pathetic scene. There was none who did not shed a tear when the dead body was put on a funeral pyre.

Bhola and Vicky went again on the third day when the community gathered for mass condolescence. Silence was observed for two minutes and everybody offered rose petals on the picture of Mohan Singh kept on a pedestal. Then all people who had gathered went to the temple and the priest sprinkled water and gave a piece of basil leaf to eat. The relatives of Mohan Singh stood in a row outside the temple and everyone passed from before them as a final expression of sharing the grief.

In the evening Vicky received a message from father of Mohan Singh to meet him next day morning. Bhola returnred to his duty when Vicky went to meet father of Mohan Singh popularly called Thakur Saab. He was sitting with brothers and were sharing Hukka. Thakur Saab told him that Mohan Singh has made a will and he wants Vicky and Kiran to take care of the institute.

Already institution had gained reputation at state level due to best academician and educationist in the Board of Director.Vicky was to work as CEO of Education wing and Kiran would be CEO of Technical wing which will work separately. Mohan Singh had incorporated aTrust in the honour of his great grand father Jaswant Singh who was once appointed as Chairman of the Contonement Committee due to his command on English.

Mohan Singh had made all arrangements to run the institutions smoothly. Vicky did not believe the offer. He said to Thakur that he is not mature enough to bear the responsibilities of the post. Thakur said he trusted the decision of his son.

Thakur said there is one stipulation in the will.It says you will have to marry Kiran and only in that case both of you would be given this responsibility. The option will remain open to you both for five years or the marriage of either one of you, whichever is earlier. Vicky took a sigh of relief, since he had time to consider all aspects of the proposal.

Next day morning he rang up Kiran and told her everything about death and will of Mohan Singh. She was stunned to hear the news. All eventualities despite their certainity, surprises.

"Why Me"? she almost shrieked on phone surprised by sudden inherItance.

"I don't know, may be you are his best conquest that he wants to reward for" Vicky said, but he immediately regretted having passed such a crude remark to Kiran. So he immediately recapitulated and said " He wants to see both of us happy out of his guilt" Vicky paused "After all, we could be deserving it"

That put a lotion on the bruised ego of Kiran. She said they had enough time to decide their future course of action, so when the time would come they would make a right choice.

Then she asked if it was painful for him to die.

Vicky looked at the watch for talking on ISD call was a costly affair, he said goodnight as it was going to be night in USA and puts his phone off.

Moreover, Kiran's concern over Mohan Singh always irritated him. Does she want to draw some pleasure in the details of his death? All deaths are painful, for someone or the other. The intensity of pain is highest when the deceased is a young person. Whole society mourn the death as if to repent that would enjoy all the amusements granted by God for many more years even when the deceased would not be with us, and after few years we would stop missing him.

"What is the use of that rememberance that becomes fade with the passage of time till one day you are lost in oblivion." Vicky pondered. One feels ashamed for having forgotten the date of demise of the person they thought they can not live one day without.Who gave this power to time, to heal those wounds which were necessary for survival? The guilt of living and enjoying the life without them is fatal and despirited. They too depart from the world leaving a vaccum behind for further guilt ridden people. That's a horrible vicious cycle. Vicky found himself trapped since the day he saw that nightmare.

Vicky had consciously avoided the thought of nightmare . Everytime it came back more vividly. Vicky was constantly haunted by the body of caterpillar with the face of Mohan Singh begging to save him from the cluthches of death. If possible Vicky would have given his life to save Mohan Singh. Only if God of death was broad minded, he would permit this kind of swapping. But he is cruel, obstinate, orthodox and traditional. The good qualities of punctuality and discipline that we usually adore in others, make him more horrible. The only consolation is that he does not discriminate on any ground and one can not beg a moment extra when he decides to take him away.

The center of the pain of the death is not body but mind. The first thing people do is to take the sufferer to a hospital or a doctor. This whole medical humbug is a big camouflage to hide the hypocracy of the society. It is a way to show the concern, an effort to reduce the pain and prolong the sufferings rather than allowing the sufferer to depart in peace. Vicky nauseated at the sight of all types of medical gadgets with tubes and IV sets attached to the patient. Given a chance he would never prefer to die like that. In town old people died at home, surrounded by siblings. That made death more tolerable. To see your own refelection in the eyes of siblings made you feel immortl , which makes pain of death tolerable.

Did Mohan Singh come to him that day seeking immortality. Vicky could put the institution made by Mohan Singh on world map and that would make Mohan Singh immortal. He wants to turn the dreams of children convert into a reality and see his own reflection in their eyes when those dreams come true.

Vicky knew later or sooner he would have to take up the project, but to marry Kiran for that was an impossibility. He was not yet mentally prepared for marriage. Though the past of Kiran or her inability to bear an offspring would not affect his decision to marry her. How a person can be penalized for the crime committed against him or her. They could adopt a child from orphanage or may be it would be better to treat all children who studied in school as their own children.

This thought brought a smile on the face of Vicky, he had already started making plan about his married life with Kiran.

Due to forthcoming elections the city administration was shuffled.

The new collector and District Magistrate was a young and dynamic officer of Indian Civil Services. His name was Sudhir Gupta, and he was handsome and bachelor. Soon he became popular due to his sober nature and zeal to resolve the issues. His mentor a Professor in the University was also the relative of Shalini's father. The professor told Sudhir that he must contact the family . Sudhie saw no harm in it. Usually cultured people never ask for undue favours, give an honest feedback and genuinely regard the authority.

The Superintendent of Police was Bhanu Pratap Singh. He was promoted from provincial police service and was honest and hard worker. Many criminals left the city when they heard that Bhanu Pratap Singh is new S.P. of the district. The pickpockets, bootleggers, chain snatchers, vehicle thieves, eveteasers, drugpeddlers, either became underdround or were caught and deported to other districts.

It was rumoured that few years back the Police Officer caught his own daughter with her boyfriend in a curtained cabin of restaurant popular amongst youth for privacy. Since that day he had become an arch enemy of illicit love affairs of youth. He would catch all couples from public places, cabins and farm houses and would call the parents of the girl and the boy. He would mishandle and beat the boy, cut his all hairs to make him bald and snatch their mobiles to check for porn photos and videoclips. That would cause humiliation before parents and society. Many girls were of marriagible age and their parents were scared that any rumour about the character of their daughter would spoil her prospective marriage.

Soon all public places, parks, hotels and restaurant were deserted and no couple was ever detected. The parents of young girls took a sigh of relief, since their daughters were mostly at home and stopped leaving home on an excuse of extra classes at odd hours, or for frequent birthday parties of the friends.

S.P. came to know that age of flirtation had gone down and even school girls bunk the school and go to hotels which provide them cloakroom facilities to dump school bag and change school uniform. They would wear modern clothes and cover their face with long scarf af if to save the facial skin from strong sunrays, but in fact it served the purpose of concealing their identity from any acquaintance who may notice and report it to their parents. The girls were minor and gravity of offence was higher, but at the same time the future of children was also at stake. S.P.used law to reform the people and not to destroy their lives.

Despite the best intentions of S.P. lives were destroyed. Being thief is different from being caught as thief. Society punishes only those who are caught. It depends on caution and destiny, and Sanjana Mishra was running low on both the fronts. Since most of her friends were Rajput boys who boasted their close proximity with Police department and the new S.P. was also a Rajput from the neighboring district, she was sure her activities are far and beyond the reach of the police.

Just at the outskirt of the city one Rajput boy had made a beautiful farm house. It had very big campus and a tube well and even a small hillock. The farm house had all the amenities of a five star hotel. Sanjana was fond of Jacuzzi and swimming. Due to high boundry wall and fear of Banna nobody dared to come closer to the farm house. Sanjana loved to walk nude in the shadows of the tree and swim in the pool. She did not mind being alone with five boys. They were all handsome and powerful, physically, financially and socially.

That day they had given her a golden wrist watch, and she was willing to reward them with every penny worth of it.

But destiny had other rewards for her. Rich and powerful people have secret enemies. Either they are victims of whims and cynics of rich or are jealous. One such fellow tipped the police. S.P. made squad to raid the place. They crossed the boundry wall and walked behind trees upto farm house. The group of five nude boys and one girl were playing water games in the pool. They had brought videographer from the department to shoot the entire episode. When Police surrounded them and asked to surrender they could not believe it.

They protested, gave references of high political and administrative connections, but police did not care. Their mobiles were seized so that police action is not intervened. The one who leaked to police also leaked to press. Consequently there were about dozen journalist and camera men to shoot the whole event. When they were arrested and asked to sit in the police jeep they covered there faces to avoide defamation by press. Sanjana fainted few times when a female police constable caught her wrist mercilessly. She tried to bite her hand that infuriated the female constable and she hit her hard on the face. Sanjana fainted and when she was conscious again she did not protest at all.

One Rajput boy who was son of a local MLA was most aggressive. His father was very powerful in political lobby of Chief Minister. He threatened S.P. for immediate transfere. He took out his revolver and fired in the air. Police was taken aback for a moment and he ran behind the trees. Two police officers ran after him, but he was young quick and desparate, and he also knew a secret entry in the boundrywall of the farm house so he escaped. All this was recorded on video and by press. Four boys and Sanjana were taken to Police Station.

All news paper and TV channels broadcasted the news. Soon every one in the city knew who the boys and girl were? The parents of Sanjana refused to come to police station to rescue her. They even said that she was not their daughter. Ultimately an NGO came forward to bail her out. When she was in police lockup and S.P. had gone, the female constable spread the news that she tried to bite her. She was showing the mark of her teeth on the back of her palm. The sub inspector called her in his room to interrogate.

In the interrogation Sub-Inspector asked her vulgre questions in abusive language and she felt humiliated beyond her tolerance. Police had recovered the golden wrist watch and the photographs were enough to prove that she was involved in immoral traffic. Then she was taken to Medical Jurist for examination. Unfortunately Dr. Saraswat was a friend of her father and had made some passes in the past. Once when she was alone he even fondled her breast and she had threatened to complaint her parents. He was also General Secretary of the Brahaman Mahasabha, which was their community organization. Only one female constable was present, who already cautioned doctor that the girl is out of control. Doctor said he knew how to handle such girls.

What he did in the name of medical examination was worst than a rape. Sanjana had cried whole night after interrogation, so when doctor caused pain by TFT and in collecting specimen, she tried to cry but no tears came. Her tear glands had gone empty by pumping tears whole night. The female contable also enjoyed her torture by the doctor and when doctor was satisfied that he had taken maximum advantage of the situation he left her bereft of any self prestige.

When she was produced before magistrate, he granted her bail. The parents refused to talk to her and asked her to leave home with her lugagage. She went to her room and tried to collect few clothes in a small suitcase. But where would she go? She was sure nobody would give her asylum. When she was packing her clothes she came across her favourite black colour black chunni used with salwar kameez. She looked at the height of ceiling fan and length of chunni and made a decision.

Most of the people do not have enough courage to live a life without reputation.

Though Vicky had met her only once but he was impressed by her beauty and sensuality. Such a tragic end of beautiful poem was a waste of art, Death had again confronted him with a blow,and he had no choice but to accept the supremecy of death over life.

Since the spirit of cursed cat had left her body, Usha had calmed down and had lost her apitite for any adventures. She spent most of the time in listening spiritual channels on TV and bhajans on her DVD player. She observed many fast and spent hours conducting rituals to please Krishna. She heard about Sanjana and felt pity for her friend. She prayed God to put her soul at peace.

Not many people came for condolescence to the parents of Sanjana, and after a few days they behaved as if she was not born. There was no picture of her in the house and all her belongings were distributed amonst the poors. There was nothing in the house to remind anyone that Sanjana, the Goddess Venus, once lived in this house.

Sudhir Gupta the Collector and District Magistrate invited the family of Kiran's father on a cup of tea. Shalini was a pleasant surprise for Sudhir. Professor had told nothing about Shalini, otherwise he would have invited earlier. Whereas, Sudhir was anticipating a bore afternoon with an old couple , the family was full of entertainment. The father of Shalini told anecdotes about his experience in Indian Railways in a hilarious way.

Shalini recited poems of John Milton, her own poems and sung a song in local dilect. Sudhir was highly impressed by the cultured family and saw Shalini as prospective life partner. He decided to consider the possibility with open mind, inquired about girl and took her consent before talking to her parents and his own parents. The face of Shalini , her smile, simplicity, mannerism haunted him whole night. In the morning he talked with his mother. She could notice the change in his voice and before he could protest, she announced that she is coming to meet him.

He had to confess about his cause of turmoil. His mother was pleased to see that her son who always boasted of taking no interest in girls was finally shy like a teenager when he talked about Shalini. His mother decided that they would go to her house to ask for Shalini. A meeting was arranged and sudden arrival of parents of Sudhir followed by quick meeting was an indirect message which parents of grown up children can easily read.

Parents of Shalini were sure that due to their family background, they would get a good match for her, but that he would be a collector and that the proposal would come from their side was beyond imagination for them.

Even ten million was not enough dowry in the trade community for a Collector. Shalini's father had hardly one million rupees saved for the marriage of Shalini. He slipped this information when he noticed that mother of Sudhir was behaving as if Shalini is already her bahu. The parents of Sudhir immediately told that money is not at all criterion and Sudhir earns enough money to live a good life.

Everybody consented and betrothal was arranged same day. In the night Shalini sent an SMS to Vicky, that she was now engaged to Sudhir, the collector of the district and she is destroying her SIM of mobile phone. When Vicky replied with congrates the message was not delivered since the number was unreachable.

Though Shalini and Vicky were not committed , Vicky had a hope when Shalini attended to his parents in the marriage of Megha. But again he knew that Sudhir was far better option for Shalini than him in all respect, so he should not regret that his friends had acted wisely.

He would sit in his rocking chair with an opened book in his hands, but he would not read a single word and gaze at wooden box with empty cocoon for hours.

It is better to be empty than filled. Every attempt to fill emptiness made him more hollow. The one for whom he wove this shell had walked out. He could not stop it from going. Once it was the sole purpose of his existence. Now when he is left alone he enjoyed a type of freedom he never thought existed.

THE END